The Long Arm of the Mounted

The Long Arm of the Mounted

by WILLIAM BYRON MOWERY

Illustrated by STEPHEN J. VOORHIES

WHITTLESEY HOUSE
MCGRAW-HILL BOOK COMPANY, INC.
New York : Toronto

THE LONG ARM OF THE MOUNTED

Copyright, 1948, *by* WILLIAM BYRON MOWERY

All rights reserved. This book, or parts thereof, may not be reproduced in any form without the permission of the publisher.

PUBLISHED BY WHITTLESEY HOUSE
A DIVISION OF THE MCGRAW-HILL BOOK COMPANY, INC.

Printed in the United States of America

Contents

The Mystery of the Ghost Gold	7
Mannikin Talk	67
A Relic of the Vikings	83
Shepherd of the Storm	101

The Mystery of the Ghost Gold

David met Esther on the path beyond the barracks.

*I*N THE DROWSY quiet of that August afternoon, Sergeant David Kirke, lying on the buffalo grass behind the Mounted Police barracks, heard someone suddenly call out his name.

"Sergeant Kirke! Sergeant David Kirke! Where in consternation are you, Dave?"

Wondering what Constable "Dusty" Goff wanted of him, the tall, rangy sergeant closed the book which had lain in front of him unread and called back, into the quadrangle of Police buildings, "Here, Dusty."

As he waited for the constable to come around the barracks, his gray eyes, troubled and uneasy, rested upon the massive Rockies a hundred miles westward. Under the evening sun the prairie and wild Alberta foothills were bluish hazy, as though from the camp smoke of Indian bands and the dust of the great shaggy herds that were vanishing from the Canadian Plains. But the towering Rockies, reaching out of sight to the north and south, stood out above the haze, stark and clear.

Constable Goff came breezing around the corner.

"Looky, sarge, Inspector Haley wants to see you in his cabin. I think he's got your furlough papers and your leave pay ready."

"Thanks, Dusty."

Constable Goff lingered a moment. "This furlough of yours, Dave—where're you spending it? Back East at your home, I'd guess. Been a long time since you've seen your people."

David winced a little. Yes, it had been a long time, a long and pleasureless time, since he had seen the Eastern cities. It seemed endless years that he'd been watching over Indian bands, shepherding homesteaders, keeping track of prospectors and trappers, and being the long arm of the law in that frontier country. He had wanted desperately to get home that summer, before it was too late—to see his mother once again and shake his dad's hand. But now he knew that this was not to be.

Goff hurried back to the Police quadrangle, where he and another off-duty constable were tossing turnips in the air and practicing "dry shooting" with their revolvers. For a few moments longer the sergeant stood looking westward toward the white-capped giants of the Great Divide. With the low slant sun inching down behind them, the lofty peaks of the Rockies were flinging long shadows far out across the rolling plains and making queer darkish shapes in the summer-evening clouds. Now the shadows would seem like covered wagons lumbering across the prairie; now like Piegan warriors on their ponies, sullenly watching the caravan

The Mystery of the Ghost Gold 13

of the pioneers; now like the lone sentinel figure of a Mounted horseman, watching both the red hunter and the homesteading white man.

As David started around for Inspector Haley's cabin, he came upon a middle-aged Blood Indian squatting on his heels at the side door of the barracks. It was Itai-Po, the Moon-Shadow, whom the Police detachment had been using as a scout for their patrols into the mountain fastnesses to the west.

Clad in breechclout and moccasins, Itai-Po was no reservation Indian but thoroughly a son of the Plains and the great Strong-Woods of Alberta. For weapons he carried only a knife and a short ram's-horn bow, wound with a rattlesnake skin. The blanket across his shoulders was a Stikine River *narhkin*, woven of bighorn wool and decorated with the Snake and Magic Crane of the North Fox totem.

As the Indian rose up facing him, David said, "You remember yesterday, Itai-Po, I said you'n me might pitch off together again? On a *hiyu* big scout this time."

Itai-Po's black eyes lit up with the adventure of spruce-shadowed trails and man-hunting with the lean, quiet sergeant.

David went on, "Good. This evening we pitch off. We leave *hyas* quick—in half a pipe. You ready, huh?"

"I been wait," Itai-Po answered. "Where go, mebbe? Peace River? Sikanni River? What work, mebbe? Patrol?"

David jerked his thumb to the northwest. "We go

there. No patrol. We go *stoh lepee neiska*—on our own hook. You wait here two-three minutes for me, Itai-Po."

He went on to Inspector Haley's cabin, knocked, and walked in. The officer, elbow-deep in paper work at his desk, answered David's salute and reached for two envelopes.

"Here's your furlough, Kirke," he said, holding out the larger envelope. "And here"—the smaller envelope, with the dull jingle of gold coins—"is your means of enjoying it. I sincerely hope you have the fine, refreshing leave you deserve."

David folded the furlough papers carefully into his money-belt and dropped the gold coins into his pocket. "This leave," he remarked, "is only for a month, sir—"

Inspector Haley looked at him blankly. "*Only?*" he echoed. "Why, Division Headquarters issued an order that no officer or man is to get more than two weeks, Kirke. I nearly perjured myself to get you 'only a month.' I felt you've been working too hard too long. You've done two terms out here on the Plains without one free day."

"I'm grateful to you, sir," David said. "Ordinarily I'd be ashamed to ask for still more time. But I simply can't get back here by the fifth of September."

"Why not?"

David looked away, out the window. "I'd just as soon not say, now. It might seem like a wild-goose chase."

"But you're visiting your home in the East, aren't you?"

"I've had to give that up."

Haley looked at him narrowly. "Are you sure you can't tell me where you're going and what you'll be doing? I'm speaking not as your superior officer but as your friend. You know how serious the penalties are for overstay."

David slowly nodded. "I know. I'll take what comes."

Haley thrummed on the desk a moment. "Well, I'll do what I can for you. If you simply can't get back by the fifth of September, and any question comes up, I'll state that you're on a secret patrol to the Okanagan."

David shook his head. "That's mighty fine of you, sir, but I won't let you risk a marred record for my sake."

"That's my concern. There's just one thing I'm asking of you—to get back here and wipe the McPherson killing off our slate before winter sets in. Headquarters has been riding me to get that murder cleaned up. The case has been all yours so far, so you're the one to finish it off."

David asked, "What if it can never be finished?"

Haley cleared his throat uneasily. "Kirke, I want to ask you a frank question. Do you think that Esther Shannon and her brother had any connection with this murder? I know that you—uh—saw Esther Shannon pretty steady this summer. You are better acquainted at their place than anybody else; you've done all the investigating on this case, so your opinion ought to be authentic."

David winced at the question. He finally said, "Esther

and Paul were given a jury trial and acquitted for lack of proof, weren't they, sir?"

"That trial," Haley remarked impatiently, "didn't prove anything. The court had no facts except what you presented, and that's why I want your own private opinion. Do you think that the Shannons had some connection with this murder—yes or no?"

"In a serious charge like murder, sir, an opinion without bedrock proof is not only useless but wrong. To voice such an opinion aloud is little short of criminal."

"But see here," Haley objected, "opinion is all we Police have to go on, nine times out of ten. Opinion is what led you to investigate the Shannons and dig up evidence against them—"

"Sir, that evidence came to light by itself; I didn't dig it up. I went to the Shannon place because a clue, not an opinion, led me there."

"Then why under heaven did you recommend that the Shannons be arrested and given a public trial? You've handled enough cases to know that your facts wouldn't convict in this instance, where the extreme penalty would have been levied. The Shannons told a flimsy story, I know, and the evidence against them was strong, but I personally would have had to be absolutely sure before I'd have brought them to trial. And I wasn't friendly with them, as you were."

Kirke listened patiently. In those days since the trial he himself had more than once doubted if he had done the wise thing. It was no clear-cut issue, one way or other. But always he had come back doggedly to the conviction that he had done right.

Haley went on, "It's true that the Shannons were acquitted, Kirke, but you dragged them into that trial and so you ought to feel responsible for getting back here as soon as possible and finding that killer. Acquittal or no, they'll be under a cloud until you do that. Will you have a mailing address where I can reach you if anything new comes to light about this case?"

David smiled a little, grimly. "A mailing address—where I'm going? Hardly!" He noticed Haley's puzzled frown and added, "I'm not hiding anything willfully, sir. The truth is, I myself don't know exactly where this business will take me or what I'll be doing."

"*Hmmph!* Well, can I help you in any way? Extra money? Personal backing?"

David turned to leave. "You might keep an eye on the Shannons, sir. Paul isn't strong, you know, and Esther—well, she just doesn't belong in a raw country like this."

"I'll watch out for them both," Haley promised. He reached out his hand. "Good luck and Godspeed—wherever you're going."

David shook hands, saluted, then turned and walked out of the cabin.

A few steps from the door Itai-Po was waiting for him. David asked, "You got our canoe ready, Itai-Po?"

The Blood pointed at a clump of whitewoods along the bank of Bear River, a quarter mile west of the post. "Canoe tied up there. My light birchrind."

"Good. How about your camping outfit?"

The Indian tapped a small pack he carried. It was not much larger than a folded blanket. "*Hiyu* many portages," he explained. He pointed at a long-tailed magpie that was flying over the barracks and having an awkward time in the evening breeze. "Fool bird carry heap big tail and go *flap-flap*; hummer bird tote little tail and go *zip*."

David smiled. "Right. Now listen, Itai-Po. You go put canoe to water and paddle up Bear River to landing at Shannon place. I go there by horse. We meet there at dusk and pitch off. You *kumtux?*"

Itai-Po nodded and started toward the whitewoods. David went into the barracks and crossed to the boarded-off corner that was his room.

His preparations were brief and hasty. He took off his uniform, laid it away in the locker, and put on civilian khaki. Into his pack went a light fishing outfit, a few articles of clothing, two pairs of moccasins, his Service binoculars, extra ammunition for his belt-gun and Enfield rifle, and two tight-woven blankets to wrap it all in.

Dusty Goff sauntered in and stood watching. "Not wasting any time getting away, I see, Dave. Where are you heading for? Looks like a bush trip of some sort."

"Might be," David evaded.

Dusty remarked, "If it wasn't that I ain't seen you spending any evenings at the Shannon place lately, I'd guess you might be pitching off on your honeymoon."

The remark cut David like a knife. But he said nothing and went on with his preparations. From his locker he took a battered felt hat and a patched old corduroy coat and stowed them carefully in his pack.

"Snakes," Goff remarked, "them ain't duds for a honeymoon, if you *are* off on a honeymoon. But with quiet fellers like yourself, you never cain tell what they're up to."

David whirled around, an angry order on his lips. But he managed to fight it back. "Dusty," he said quietly, "go out and saddle a horse for me, will you? I'll be riding for a few miles on this trip. Then I'll send the horse back. Keep an eye out for it after supper."

"Surelee will, if you say so," Dusty agreed. "But you know it brings bad luck to send your horse home with the saddle on. When that happens, the Crees say, it means you won't ever come back from that trip."

"That's not the worst thing I can imagine," Kirke said cryptically. "No, not the worst. . . ."

2

In the first hush of evening he left the Police post on the chestnut gelding that Dusty had saddled for him and headed northwest over the park-prairie country, cutting across a bend of the Bear River. The region was at the far northern wash of the homesteader wave, and it looked as lone and deserted as when it had been a battleground between the Bloods and Assiniboins, not so many years ago. Three miles from the post he rode past a small nester place in a creek bottom—the only settler sign in his hour's ride.

Four miles beyond the nester place he struck the bank of the Bear River, just below the great bend where the stream swung abruptly west and headed straight for the distant foothill wilderness. Through the riverbank whitewoods and birches he rode out into a small clearing where a gravel creek flowed into the Bear.

In the middle of the clearing stood a rambling, split-log building of several rooms, with a small empty stable at the woods edge, a fur-cache dugout, a springhouse, and a canoe landing. Built by Esther Shannon's uncle in the year when David had first come to that region, the place had been intended as a trading post and overnight lodging for trappers, homesteaders, and prospectors. But the homesteader wave had failed to come, travelers were few, and the tiny post had never panned out.

The twilight river, the creeping prairie roses around the clearing, and the piney tang drifting down from the low hills up the creek brought David poignant memories of the evenings he had gone walking in the whippoorwill dusk with Esther Shannon. He hated to think of the long weeks when he would be away and she would be almost by herself there. The spot was so lonely for human habitation. Lonely, wild, and isolated.

He took his rifle from the saddle-bucket, lifted off his pack, and turned the horse around. At his sharp command to "home," the Police mount started back toward

The Mystery of the Ghost Gold 21

the post at a brisk canter. Leaving his rifle and pack near the canoe landing, David walked up the path toward the split-log building.

In the small garden near the springhouse Esther Shannon was gathering an apronful of peas for the evening meal. As David drew near, she heard him coming, turned, and he was face to face with her, for the first time since the murder trial at Bear River Settlement.

A graceful, medium-tall girl of twenty-three, with soft brown hair and warm brown eyes, Esther Shannon had come from the East, like David, and the East still clung to her. It was always a marvel to him that this girl should be living in that raw, pioneer region. Her family had homesteaded in the Moose Jaw district several years ago; her parents had died in a prairie blizzard, and she had been thrown entirely on her own, with a younger brother to look after. For two years she had taught a Mission school in Saskatchewan, then the half-breed school at Bear River Settlement. On the death of her uncle, who had homesteaded this tract along the Bear River and staked a float-gold claim up the tributary creek, she had come there to live out the two remaining years of the Crown requirement and nurse her brother Paul back to health.

It had been a bad mistake—but she had not known this beforehand. The gold claim had proved worth little; the expected settler tide had kept far to the south; the life had been dreadfully lonesome and bleak for her. In his quiet way David had tried to watch over the Shannon place and buoy her up through the bad times. But then, as the last and worst of all her troubles, the McPherson incident. . . .

As David confronted her now, he was shocked at the deep weariness on her sweet young face. Uncertain how she would receive him, he touched his hat and said awkwardly, "I meant to call around sooner, Esther, but I had extra work to clean up before my furlough."

She did not answer. David noticed the coldness in her manner, so different from what it had been that spring and early summer. She was looking at him as though he were a stranger. Or worse—an enemy.

He picked up the wooden pail of vegetables she had gathered and said, "I'll carry it for you," and they went out along the gravel path to the kitchen door. Esther stopped there, not inviting him inside. David set the pail just over the threshold and stood fumbling his hat. Finally he explained.

"I'm going away on furlough, Esther. For several weeks. I came past to say good-by—and to see you." Then he remembered her book that he had, and took it out of his jacket pocket. "And to return this, too."

Still Esther said nothing. In the silence he heard her brother Paul down on the creek-bank trail, evidently coming home.

He tried again to probe into what she was thinking and feeling toward himself. "When I get back, sometime in September—would you lend me that book again, Esther? I thought to finish it this afternoon, but—"

She interrupted him. "If you really want to finish the book, Sergeant Kirke, you'd better keep it now. I won't need it any more."

David was jarred by her words. As plain as daylight, she was saying that she did not intend ever to let him see her again.

He scuffed at the gravel with his boot and plunged into the subject that lay between them. "Heaven knows you've reason to be bitter about that trial, Esther. But I was hoping you'd withhold judgment till I could talk with you and explain—"

Again she cut him short. "I think that the trial spoke for itself, Sergeant Kirke. Nothing that can be said now would recall one word or one moment of that dreadful experience. I wish you wouldn't bring the subject up again."

"But don't you see, Esther, that I acted under compulsion? I had reasons for causing the arrest and the trial."

Esther tossed her head angrily. "Of course you had. Good reasons, to your way of thinking. When some silly clue pointed to this place, you felt it was your duty to follow that clue. You'd been welcomed here as a friend, and because of that, you were able to unearth other alleged evidence against us. That also, I suppose, was your duty. And then, as an officer of the law, you were simply compelled to drag us into the glare and shame of a trial for murder!"

David tried again to explain. "That open trial, Esther,

was safer than to let rumor and dangerous talk go on till it got out of hand. You and Paul were suspected by everyone in this district—"

"Including yourself!" Esther interrupted, her low tones passionate with anger. "Otherwise you'd have had the courage to stand between us and arrest. And now you're going away on a pleasure trip—now of all times!—and letting Paul and me bear this hateful suspicion."

Under her bitter indictment David stood silent and miserable, realizing the utter hopelessness of any explanation. Yet he felt that no man could let charges like hers go unchallenged, and finally he said, "Whether you believe me or not, Esther, I did *not* use my welcome here to spy on you and Paul. You mustn't say things like that, which can never be unsaid."

Instead of answering him, Esther turned and went into the cabin, and closed the door in his face.

As David slowly turned away and went down the path, he met Paul Shannon coming up from the creek trail.

The nesters and half-breeds thereabouts pitied Paul Shannon because he was a "lunger," but their pity was mixed with contempt—a young man of twenty who could not chop down a tree or ride a bronc or hold a plow in the prairie sod. But Kirke had early realized that Paul Shannon had been born for other things. There were times when he felt a little in awe of the lad's dreaming, visionary nature. And he knew that Esther, too, understood the quality of genius in her young, stricken brother, and this had made her fight for him all the fiercer.

David noticed the boy's muddied trousers and said, "You've been tom-rocking up on that claim, Paul. That's too hard for you. Didn't you and I have a private agreement that when you needed a bit of money to tide over, you'd let me lend it to you?"

"I didn't think an hour or two at the claim would hurt any," Paul said in his dreamy way. He put down his shovel and mattock as a spell of coughing came on, and leaned weakly against a sapling. "But I guess—it did—hurt, David."

David put a steadying hand on his shoulder, badly shaken by the boy's paleness and his indomitable courage. "Paul," he said, when the worst of the coughing was over, "I'm going away for a few weeks, and while I'm gone I'll want to know that you're not tom-rocking float or doing any other work you shouldn't. Here"—he reached into his pocket for the gold coins of his furlough pay and put them into Paul's hand—"that'll tide you over. Just don't let on about it to Esther, for heaven's sake. She doesn't understand about that trial. I hope you do."

"I know you were trying somehow to be our friend," Paul said. "It was like walking through a dark woods at night, with you guiding us and fighting off dangers." He looked at the gold in his hand and slowly shook his head. "But I can't accept this, David. No, I can't."

"Why not? It's just a loan. You've taken other little loans from me."

"That was when I felt sure I could pay you back. But this—I know I won't be able to repay you."

David thought the boy was losing his courage and giving up his dogged fight for life. He argued, "Nonsense, Paul! You're starting to pick up. After a winter here in these pine hills you'll be hard as nails. You mustn't be discouraged. That's letting Esther down. Of course you'll pay me back; keep that money, please."

"It's not that I'm discouraged," Paul explained. "It's that—well, we won't be here, David."

"*What?*"

"We're going to leave here," Paul added. "Esther has started to pack up already. We're going out of this country entirely and going back East. It's too hard a fight to hang on till the land becomes ours."

It seemed to David that all his plans came crashing about his ears. A little dazed, he stood there fighting to think; fighting down a rebellion against the thankless role he had been forced to play and the raw injustice to himself. What was the use, he asked, of going ahead with the long dangerous trip he had planned? When he got back, this Shannon place would be deserted, and Esther would be half a continent away.

Out of the deepening twilight he saw Itai-Po's slender birchbark come gliding silently in toward the canoe landing. The sight of it reminded him again of his plans, his duty, and the long spruce-shadowed trail ahead. He shook Paul's hand and said good-by, and went out the path for his pack and rifle.

At the landing he stepped into the canoe and shoved it off. They swung out into the current and headed west, toward the foothills and the mountains on beyond.

3

The days that followed were long, and each like the other. Dawn broke at three in the morning, and at ten at night there was still paddling light on the bosom of lake or river. At the earliest gray of morning, when the solitaire was singing his *"Lévé! Lévé!* Come alive!" David was out of his blankets and whipping a pool for trout. By the time he returned with four or five, Itai-Po would have his cone of fire built and camp ready to be broken. In twenty minutes they were through with breakfast, into the canoe, and gone.

Every two hours they stopped for a pipe, and three times during the long day for a mug-up. They carried no food, but relied on berries, fish, waterfowl, and occasionally a black-tailed deer or woodland caribou at a lake edge. At each camp Itai-Po produced a gum-pot and smeared cracks in his birchbark.

The foothills themselves ran through cycles that were as regular as the days. First it was the silent river, winding through forests of columnar spruce; then a river-widening or valley lake, aflutter with teal, ducks, geese, and the sonorous trumpeter swan; then a gushing, white-water creek at the upper end, leading up to a tiny watershed over some hill range; then portage, white-water creek, lake, and the spruce-buried river again.

The two of them had silence in common, and they passed hours without so much as grunting at each other. Itai-Po's expertness at canoe work and David's strength and stamina made a unique water-dogging combination. Their swift pace was a reassurance to David, whose furlough days were precious, and it brought a keen satisfaction to the wilderness-loping Itai-Po. Their "pipes," the Blood said, were the longest he had ever known in canoe travel. When they covered in two days a distance which the swiftest Assiniboin runner had never covered in less than three, Itai-Po's swarthy face cracked in a derisive grin at besting the ancient enemies of his tribe.

For the sake of speed they were constantly taking white-water *sautes* which looked like suicide and scudding straight across wind-swept lakes instead of following the shore line. They poled up rapids, towed through gorges, and short-cut over the padded trails of moose and caribou.

When Bear River shallowed into a foothill brook, they portaged through six heart-breaking miles of new windfall to the nearest canoe water, and sped on, range after range, till they dropped down into the broad valley of Mountain River, a steely, snow-fed stream that wound between the foothills and the Rockies.

So far they had followed the centuries-old trade route between the Coastal Siwash and the Indians of the

Great Plains; but at Mountain River the route bent south a hundred miles to an easy pass across the Great Divide.

"Too slow, that trade route; we waste days," David said. On a sand bar he sketched a map and indicated a point on the far side of the Divide. "We want to go there, Itai-Po. You get us there quick as quick can."

For half an hour the Indian squatted on his heels and studied the map. Finally he said, "No man ever go straight through. But *we* go straight through. It five sleeps quicker than follow trade path."

That evening they laid their canoe away in a cave, and the next morning they lifted their packs and began the climb up the eastern slope of the Divide.

For nearly half the distance there they followed an old moccasin trail which the Chilcoots had used on their big-horn hunts and their raids against the Blackfeet. It took them steadily higher and higher, with few dips into the canyons. The trail dimmed to nothingness, but Itai-Po pushed boldly ahead, with a surety that amazed David. They made lean-to shelters of limber-pine branches at night, and put moss into their moccasins against the jagged stones and increasing cold; and David kept his rifle free to guard against the huge lumbering silvertips.

They climbed out of the hardwoods into the big conifers, where the gray crow was at home; out of these into the storm-gnarled tamarack and ground pines; then up across the heather terraces, which were vivid splashes of red and yellow flowers, with innumerable butterflies playing over the heather. Above these terraces they came abruptly into the high snowlands, where the wind was keen as a whiplash; where they walked through clouds and watched storms sweeping through the valleys a mile below them.

Finally they came to a level boulder field, half a mile across, with an acre-sized lake of steel-gray water in the middle of it. A small brooklet flowed out of the lake toward the east, and on the other side a brooklet flowed toward the west, and they knew they were standing on the Great Divide itself. It was a wild, elemental scene all around them, with white ptarmigan chortling among the boulders, and the plaintive whistle of the little rabbit-like picas drifting to them ventriloquially. In every direction they looked out across an immense sweep of ranges, *névés,* and endless miles of evergreen forestry.

As they dropped down the west slope they seemed to be entering a different country altogether—a warm, moist, luxuriant land. Different songsters flitted in the bushes, the trout had different markings, the stag fern and maidenhair were strange and exotic. The winds no longer carried the chill of the Mackenzie Barrens but were mild, soft chinooks, charged with the moist warmth of the Kuro Siwa.

It was David's first trip into the country of the Western slope, and his days were filled with new experiences. The weather seemed perpetually on the verge of rain, and a cloud as big as a thumbnail would bring a heavy shower. Just below timber line they ran into slender spruce which were no bigger around than a saucer, but which reached up a hundred and fifty feet. From a cave shelter, where a storm drove them, they saw stances of these spruces whipping in the gale like fields of tall grain. As they dropped down and down, they passed through timber belts where the trees towered two hundred and fifty feet high. Still lower they came to giant cedar and yellow spruce which made saplings of the timber above.

At the first sizable creek they struck, they saw a grizzly at a pool, scooping out salmon that were spent and bruised raw by their long run from the Pacific. Itai-Po remarked, "He plenty fool, that bear. Scoop out too many fish. Watch 'em flip-flop; grin. Plenty fish bring fish hawks circling. Fish hawks bring Indian. Indian shoot bear. Ha!"

"Men can be foolish, too," David observed. "Prospector tom-rocks gold. *Hiyu* gold. Throws hat in air. Yells 'Hi-yippety yip!' Bush-sneak hears. Bellies up close. Shoots man."

Itai-Po looked at him. "Mebbe prospector this McPherson man, huh?"

David shrugged. "Mebbe so. Mebbe no. We wait-see."

They followed down the headwaters creek to a small river. There the Blood struck a fresh moccasin trail, backtracked it, and found a canoe cached under some riverbank ferns. After setting the canoe to water, he tied some knots in a strip of *babische* and put the string on a flat rock, along with a fine hunting knife and a pound of trade tobacco.

"Canoe belong Caribou Indian," he explained to David. "String knots tell him we took canoe. Pay him with knife and tabac'. You *kumtux?*"

They placed a hollow rock in the canoe prow, laid in some live coals, and put damp moss on these, to make a smudge and keep the mosquito clouds away. Then they shoved off, down the unknown western river.

Forty miles downstream they came to a triple fork and here struck the old trade trail which they had followed through the foothills. Turning north on the trail, they pushed ahead all one day and night and the next day; and that evening, just fourteen days from the time they had left the Mounted post, they came to their journey's end—the point which Kirke had indicated on his sandbar map across the mountain.

At the mouth of a little creek, whose silty water whispered of gold alluvium upstream, a larch tree had been stripped of its branches, and at the top of this lobstick an old shirt fluttered conspicuously. It was a lonely prospector's way of drawing the attention of any travelers and making sure they would not go by without visiting him.

David motioned at the lobstick. "Here we find prospector called Sockeye Sullivan, Itai-Po. Here we find out if our trip is a wild-goose chase or not."

4

At Sullivan's diggings, a hundred yards up the creek, they lifted out their canoe, and David looked around at the prospector's camp in the little birch glen. It was a typical sourdough's place, with only the raw necessities of a wilderness existence: a lopsided tent, a clothesline strung between two trees, ore specimens tossed here and there, a litter of broken tools, shafts, and rusted tins, a homemade stone stove under the flap-front of the tent, a pet marmot that scurried under a log at the sight of strangers, and a freshly killed deer hanging in a bent-over birch.

At the diggings just up the creek a burly, red-whiskered man was tom-rocking away, talking to himself as he worked. Presently he paused to rest, looked around, and saw the two visitors. The shovel dropped from his hands, and he came splashing down to greet them.

"Gosh a'mighty!" he spluttered, drop-jawed in surprise. "Comp'ny! Sockeye Sullivan, you're a born lucky malemute, you are! Hello, strangers! Where might you be a-goin', and who might you—? Why, I'm a pigeon-toed coyote if it ain't Davy Kirke! Davy, you ornery dog, is't really you, or just your spook? What the billy-whilly are you a-doin' 'way over here acrost the Rockies from where you belong? My blessed eyes—hand me your front hoof, Davy, for an honest-to-goodness shake."

His joy was pathetic. He shook hands with both of them several times over and then set about rustling up a meal, all the while keeping up a flood of talk.

"You got any t'baccy, son? I'm run out. And what time of the year is't, anyway?"

"Yes, I can spare you a couple pounds of tobacco. As for the date, this is the eighteenth."

"August, I s'pose?"

"Yes," David replied in amazement.

Over their early supper he eased the talk around to the matter which had brought him across the mountains. "Still trying to find that mother lode, are you, Sockeye? This makes your fourth year. You didn't come across to Bear River post for supplies this summer, and I took a long chance on your still being here. You must have stuck close this season."

Sullivan nodded to the last question. "Mighty close. Didn't leave at all. No, I ain't found the lode yet, but the tom-rockin' here is purty rich."

"I suppose you have company often?"

"Comp'ny!" Sullivan snorted. "They ain't half a dozen people in two hundred miles. I seen one pusson in three months, I have."

"Who was he?" David asked casually.

" 'Nother sourdough. He struck a durn nice lode over in this country last spring. Was goin' out, he was, and get help. He hit acrost the mountains from here."

"So he struck it? What made him tell you about that?"

"Why, us prospectors don't keep mum to each other about our strikes. It's the claim-jumpin' gentry that we don't dass allow to get wind of any good lode or placer we find. In gold country they's always bush-sneaks around that 'ud ax a man for a goose quill of dust."

"Why didn't this other sourdough drop down west to Siwash Fork instead of crossing the mountains?"

"Wull, he was a-carryin' a nice poke out, and the Siwash Fork route has got a bad name. He was by hisself, and he didn't have no weapons 'cept a grouse gun."

Very casually David asked, "You didn't know him, did you, Sockeye? What was his name?"

"I knowed him well, Davy. He and me worked right alongside each other once, on a pair of fractions down in Kootenay. Sort of a foot-loose, homeless feller, he was. Rough-lookin' but gentle as they come. Some people they call him 'Sumdum' and others they call him 'Red.' His last name it was McPherson."

David jerked a little. But he refused to jump to conclusions, and he asked, "What sort of man was this McPherson, Sockeye? Can you describe him for me?"

"Wull, he was big and bony, and about forty year old. Harmless sort of pusson, he was, like I said."

Still David would not let himself take anything for granted. In the length and breadth of British Columbia there might well be a dozen big, bony McPhersons. The man whom Sockeye had known, and the man who'd been murdered at the Shannon place far across the Rockies, might not be the same person at all.

He reached into his pack and pulled out an old felt hat and corduroy coat which he had brought along. "Take a look at these, Sockeye. Do they mean anything to you?"

Sullivan looked at the clothes, blinked his eyes, and swore. "Why, them's the identical duds that Sumdum was a-wearin'!"

Itai-Po grunted. David put the hat and coat back into his pack. Sockeye looked from one to the other of his visitors, puzzled and frowning.

"What's up, Davy? What've you been pokin' all them questions at me for?"

David lit his pipe and said quietly, "McPherson was murdered, Sockeye. This summer. Across in my country. Just a few miles from the Mounted post."

Sullivan jumped to his feet excitedly. "You're lyin', Davy. You can't mean that. Sumdum McPherson dead —killed. . . . Why, there wa'n't a dog that'd bite him, or a man alive that didn't take to him like a brother. I don't believe it!"

"But it's true, Sockeye. I tell you, McPherson was murdered. Those holes in his coat are bullet holes. He was shot in the back, along a riverbank, one Sunday, and his body was thrown into Bear River. The party that did it is somewhere on this green earth, and I'm out to get that party."

"Who done it?" Sullivan snarled. "I'd kill him barehanded, I would."

"I had only two clues," David went on. "I learned his name from an old Telegraph Creek grub-list in his hatband; and I found a gun near where he was shot—the weapon that was used to kill him. I myself had given that gun to a family there on Bear River, the Shannons. You don't know them. They're cheechakos from the East; Esther Shannon and her younger brother.

"They told me that McPherson had spent the night, his last night on earth, at their place. They also told me that *they* had in their possession McPherson's eight thousand dollars in dust and nuggets. They said McPherson had left the gold with them because he felt he was being followed; and also that he had borrowed their rifle for that same reason. They said they hadn't heard of his getting shot or they would have reported at once about the gold."

"Sounds like a flimsy yarn to me," Sullivan interrupted. "A'mighty flimsy, I'd say."

David nodded. "That's how people over there thought. When young Paul Shannon innocently gave it away about their having the gold, the rumors began flying, and tempers started to get ugly. So I recommended that the Shannons be arrested and given trial. The evidence for a murder case was not sufficient, and they were acquitted."

"I'd have hung 'em!" Sockeye asserted flatly.

David said nothing to that. Across his mind jigged

the bitter memory of Esther Shannon closing the door in his face, and the anguishing thought that they would be gone, she and Paul, before he could possibly get back from this wilderness trip. "Let's suppose," he went on, "that the Shannons told the truth. Then somebody else killed McPherson. For what? A grudge? He didn't look to me like a man who would make enemies. For his gold? I didn't quite believe so. A simple robbery, without the danger and hullabaloo of a murder, would have been more credible. So I asked myself, exactly why was McPherson being shadowed and why was he killed?

"His poke of gold gave me an idea. It wasn't flour gold or smooth nuggets. It was rough nuggets—which meant that it hadn't washed along very far from the mother lode. It might well be lode gold itself. I reasoned that maybe McPherson had made a fine strike, had picked up what gold was handy, and then started out for help. According to what you just told me, McPherson really did make a strike. So we're on solid ground so far.

"Now, let's do a little more supposing, Sockeye. Suppose you were McPherson, and you'd just made a good strike. What would you have done?"

"I'd have busted in to a land office and had it registered. Then I'd have got me three or four good partners and hotfooted it right back here."

David nodded. "That's what any sourdough would have done. But in country this wild, with so many creeks and canyons all looking alike, how would you make sure that you'd know the way back to your Discovery claim?"

The Mystery of the Ghost Gold 39

"Why, I'd make me a map," Sockeye said. "I'd make me a birchbark map that'd take me right back to the. . . ." He broke off there, staring openmouthed at David. Finally he burst out, "Great blazes, Davy, that's it! That's why they killed Sumdum! He had a map. They didn't hanker for his poke so much; it was the map they wanted!"

"That's what I suspected. And when I examined his coat and saw where he'd sewed a secret pocket into the lining, and somebody had ripped it open, I felt pretty sure of my guess. Furthermore, this would account for their killing him. You see, they couldn't take over the Discovery unless he was safely out of the road."

"That's abs'lutely so. You've surelee figgered this business to a teedeewhack. But how did you know that Sumdum made his strike over in these parts?"

"Some more figuring," David said. "There's not much nugget gold on the east side of the Rockies, and besides, McPherson was a stranger over there. I reasoned that he'd come from somewhere across the Divide, on the old trade trail, thinking it was safer than the Siwash Fork route. So I decided to come over here with Itai-Po and look around. I counted heavily on your being acquainted with him. And you were!"

Sockeye helped himself to more of David's tobacco. "You figger this was a one-man job?"

"No. Certain features about it make me believe it was two or three men. I also believe they came back over here and are working that lode now. They'd be leery to file on it right after the killing."

Sockeye pushed his hat back and scratched at his tousled hair. "But dang it, Davy, I don't know where Sumdum's strike is at. He didn't tell me, and I didn't want him to. All I know is it was somewhere up in the Ghost Gold."

"Where and what is that?" David asked.

Sockeye jerked a thumb to the north. "It's a country up yon—a jumble of rivers, creeks, canyons, hills and every whichnot, between two big ranges. Somebody said that when the Lord got finished creatin' the earth, He hadda lot of rocks, water, broken mountains, and big timber left over, so He just chucked it all into that region to get shut of it, and that's what makes it so wild. From time to time, ever since the days of the Golden Caribou rush, they's been sourdoughs now and then drift back into that country. Usually they come out all shaky and tellin' ding-buster tales how wild it is and about its gold. They all say it's got float gold everywhere in all the gravel bars and crick beds, but they can't find any mother lodes anywhere. They say you can trace this float gold upstream to the lode it came from and then you don't find any lode. That's why they call that country the Skookum Gold or the Ghost Gold."

"How does a person get there?"

"You just follow up this river and over the watershed and you drop down into it. But if you're thinkin' of ferretin' out them killers in that country"—he shook his

The Mystery of the Ghost Gold 41

head sadly—"you'd not have a Chinyman's chance, Davy. It's the dangdest mullix of cricks, canyons, moraines, mountains, deep woods, windfall, and rocks you ever saw. Not even the Goat-Eater Ind'uns go in there. A needle in a haystack 'ud be easy huntin' compared with findin' the party as killed Sumdum."

David thought unhappily of how swiftly his furlough was draining away, and the prospect of a long hunt dismayed him. But he said doggedly, "Itai-Po and I'll find those killers. We've got to, if it takes all winter."

" 'Nother thing," Sockeye added. "They's something wrong with that country up yon. Fellers that go into the Ghost Gold come out shakin' hands with the willows. It breaks 'em. Sumdum was a bush-loper all his life and he wasn't in there long, but he was half batty when he got out to here. Me, I wouldn't go in there for all the gold you could shake a stick at. People say it's full of ha'nts and queer doin's. . . ."

5

Two full weeks later David made a lonely camp one night at a fork where two canyons led back into the eastern mountains. He cooked supper for two, then sat down to wait.

Itai-Po should have returned to the rendezvous. He had gone up the north canyon two days before, to clean up a maze of creeks leading out of a big moraine. David had taken the south canyon and ferreted it out to his complete satisfaction—and disappointment.

The two weeks had passed without yielding one sign of any recent party in the Ghost Gold. Working northwest up the trunk river, David and the Blood scout had turned into all the branch streams and followed them back to the first portage, where a party would have left signs for Itai-Po to read. But they had found nothing— no tracks or clues along either the trunk river or the branch creeks.

Claim-jumping gentry, David knew, were not ordinarily cunning enough to hide all the signs of travel and camps, and at times he doubted if the killers were in that country at all. But he had clung to the hunt grimly, pushing himself and Itai-Po to the limit. They had paddled from twilight to twilight, with only two or three hours of sleep at night. They had chopped their way at places through the piled-up, tangled windfall of centuries, and fought white waters, and felt seeping into them the loneliness and nameless fears of a country wilder and more elemental than anything they had ever imagined.

Again and again in the lonely hours of those weeks David had thought of the bitter charges that Esther had flung at him. When he had planned this long wilderness trip, it had been with the hope that he would return with evidence which would completely free her and Paul from suspicion and that she would then understand about the trial. But now he could have no hope of any such end to the trip. She would be gone. All that would remain would be the barren satisfaction of clearing up the murder of Sumdum McPherson. And even that was beginning to look like a fool's hope.

Itai-Po did not return at dark. In an hour the moon rose, and still no Itai-Po. David ate a solitary supper and sat smoking beside the fire. Sometime after midnight a shadow glided silently out of the canyon, and Itai-Po crouched down on the other side of the dying fire.

David looked sharply at the Indian's swarthy face, and his heart leaped. *"You've found 'em!"*

Itai-Po nodded. "Struck trail at dusk-time. Didn't follow to camp. We find that tomorrow. Easy. Tonight—sleep."

At dawn they hid their canoe, smoothed out all signs of their camp, and hurried up the north canyon to Itai-Po's first "find." It was a shoe track so faint and rain-obliterated that David himself would never have noticed it. At a swift pace the Indian led him on up the canyon, pointing casually to signs where David saw nothing. He had once jokingly told Inspector Haley that Itai-Po could track a rabbit across bare rock, and now it seemed to him that the Blood was almost that uncanny at tracking.

Four miles above the forks the canyon opened out into a dark, oval valley, five miles long and half a mile wide. They went cautiously now, knowing that the camp was close. A mile farther Itai-Po stopped suddenly, with a warning gesture.

Through the buckbrush David caught a glimmer of

white, the dirty white of a canvas tent. He started forward to get a better look, but Itai-Po clutched his arm.

"Mole-eye! Look!" he ejaculated in his own tongue. "A papoose could see a trap so clumsy!"

Two juniper bushes leaned almost together across the path. Between them a green cord was stretched, so that an unwary intruder would run into and break it. Cautiously Kirke and Itai-Po followed the string. It led over a rock ledge. They looked over, and then at each other.

"Huh!" the Blood snorted. "Warning! You run into string, rattle-pan drop on rock, make *hiyu* noise, warn 'em!"

"That settles another thing," David thought to himself. "No decent prospector wants to be warned *against* company. He hangs out his shirt so that folk won't miss him. That green cord means we're at the end of our trail!"

They crept away from the path and bellied through the undergrowth toward the camp. It was new-found, on a little spot thirty steps above the stream. The tent was large—a three-man affair. No one was about, but on up the valley they heard the ring of pickax against rock.

"We go see," Kirke directed.

They backed off, circled, and from a jumble of boulders and junipers, looked down upon the diggings. The Discovery was a quartz vein at the foot of an eroded bank, which showed ten feet of gray gravel on top, then a stratum of serpentine rock, then a layer of black-rock which carried the quartz. The gravel bar in the stream

The Mystery of the Ghost Gold   45

bed was rich with free gold that had trickled out, but a short, eighteen-foot tunnel had been thrust into the hillside to follow the richer quartz vein.

Three men were working in and about the tunnel. Through his Service glasses David scrutinized them closely.

One of the trio was a *métis,* an Assiniboin half-breed. While he worked, he kept glancing sharply into the timber and rock tangles all around. His movements were furtive and sinuous, like that of a woods animal. The other two men were whites. One of them, rather small, with spindly legs and long arms, had features that suggested Oriental blood. The third was a big, bushy-whiskered man somewhat resembling Sockeye Sullivan— except that Sockeye's honesty and simple human kindness were no part of his make-up.

All three were total strangers to David. He handed the glasses to Itai-Po and said, "You know 'em?"

The Indian studied the three a little while, then lowered the binoculars. " 'Un't know two whites," he said. "But the *métis,* him Charlo Daoust. People say he once kill man over at McMurray Landing. He woods-loper, sharp as mountain cat. Twig broken, leaf upset, he see."

David nodded. The make-up of the party was clear enough. The whites were city outcasts; the 'breed was their reliance in the wilderness. His cunning was the reason why no signs had been left on the trunk-river portages.

"Look, Itai-Po," he cautioned. "This bush-wise Charlo

Daoust may find out somebody's around. That's dangerous. You're bush-wise, too. You've got to keep him from finding out. Got to show that a Blood is a better bush-shadow than an Assiniboin 'breed. You *kumtux?*"

Itai-Po nodded to the challenge. David went on.

"You and me see green cord. We know what that means. We know these men guilty. But white man's court don't know. Court won't take our yes-word. You *kumtux* what court-sure evidence means? Good. We got to get court-sure evidence. Then we arrest; not before."

Itai-Po chewed thoughtfully on a birch twig. "How get this court-sure evidence?"

It was a question easier asked than answered.

That afternoon, while Itai-Po lay watching the three men at the lode, David slipped into their camp and gave it a thorough searching. He found no map, no writing, no clues of any sort. He knew then that they had carefully destroyed every last bit of evidence connecting them with their crime. They had surely burned McPherson's map and made one of their own, and had left nothing whatever to link them with that brutal killing across the mountains last summer.

That evening, while the three were eating supper at their camp, Itai-Po slipped up to within a dozen steps and listened to their talk. It was David's hope that they would talk about McPherson and betray themselves out of their own mouths. But evidently that subject was taboo. When Itai-Po came back at the end of an hour,

The Mystery of the Ghost Gold

he reported that they had not once mentioned the killing or the prospector.

In a side canyon that evening, at the cave camp which he and Itai-Po had established, David sat up most of the night, a dead pipe in his teeth, trying to plan how he could get sure evidence against three killers who had left no evidence. He had run them down; he knew within himself that they had murdered Sumdum McPherson for this rich lode they were working; but bringing them to justice and clearing the Shannon name—that was something else again.

As he sat there, the appalling loneliness and savagery of the Ghost Gold weighed on him. The eerie wail of wind through the rock fissures and the black spruce tops, the play of moonlight shadows on the needle-carpeted moss, the distant ghostly cries of night animals—all these made him understand why the Ghost Gold had so frightening a name. He wondered—could he somehow make use of the uncanny spirit of that wild, lonely valley? Could he somehow use it to strike terror into the hearts of men whose consciences were already burdened with a murder?

6

One morning Murph Mecklin straightened up from his work and leaned for a moment on his pick handle. He looked at Greever and Daoust, who were shoveling behind him. He looked at the leaden sky and held out his hand to feel for rain.

On the north slope something cracked sharply. Mecklin whirled around to look. As his glance went up the slope, his throat split in a yelp of warning. Daoust and Greever jerked upright and would have run for their rifles, but Mecklin's second yelp and frenzied gesture stopped them. They looked.

Down the north slope a ten-ton boulder came careening straight toward them, gathering speed and lesser boulders as it rolled. For a split-wink none of the three could stir. Daoust recovered first. With the agility of a big cat he sprang toward the tunnel mouth, out of the path of the boulder. Mecklin, with Greever on his heels, hurled himself into the buckbrush and went crashing through it like a panicky bull moose.

A few seconds afterwards, with a roar that shook the ground and filled the gorge with dust of splintered rock, the boulder slide swept over the place where the three men had been working and piled up in the stream bed below, in a mass of rock and matchwood timber.

When the last trickle of gravel had subsided, the men approached the spot gingerly and eyed the destruction.

Mecklin shuddered and swore. "That was by the skin of our teeth, Greever. I heard a noise up there like a stick breakin' and looked up, and there come that roll. If I hadn't heard that crack, we'd be deader'n dirt right now! Mashed flatter'n a chip!"

"Dry up!" Greever snapped. "You blow off too much.

The Mystery of the Ghost Gold 49

Let's find what started that big boulder rollin'. It was a balancer; I seen it up there several times; but it always looked solid enough to me."

They climbed up the slope to where the big boulder had "balanced" on a pedestal of slate. The immediate cause of its toppling was plain enough; it had been hit by a smaller rock, which had bounded down the slope in ten-foot jumps and broken into fragments at the impact. But what had started that smaller one?

"Likely a grizzly huntin' for mice," Mecklin rasped. "Daoust, get busy and find his cussed tracks, and we'll shoot him."

With Daoust leading, they traced the smaller boulder up the slope into a thicket of salmonberries, and found where it had lain. Daoust looked for signs through the thicket; he circled; he came back to the boulder site, dropped on hands and knees, and searched all around.

"Well!" Greever demanded impatiently. "Where's the grizzly's tracks? Let's trail him and kill him. We don't want a hunnert tons of boulders a-pilin' down at us ever time a blasted bear gets hungry."

Daoust stood wide-legged, puzzled. "No bear signs. No bear. No signs a-tall. Nothing! I don't *kumtux*."

"Mebbe it just started rollin' natural-like," Mecklin concluded. "Let's go back and get to work cleanin' away that rock mess. We'd better cut a channel through it, or the crick'll back up into our tunnel and flood us out."

Dismissing the incident as just some freak hapchance, they went back to the lode. But all that morning and afternoon their nerves were taut and jumpy over their hairbreadth escape.

That night, as they were going down the creek to camp, a foot-log across a forty-foot chasm gave way just as Charlo Daoust, leading, stepped upon it. By a great leap backward he caught an overhanging bush and saved himself from an ugly fall down on the jagged, water-lashed rocks below.

"You built that foot-log yourself," Greever snarled at the 'breed accusingly. "You ought to've done a safe job 'stead of makin' a mantrap like that. If you'd broke your dirty neck, t'would have served you right."

"I fix foot-log good," the 'breed retorted angrily. "Good and strong. We use it two or three weeks now, and it didn't fall."

"Strong, huh? Didn't you just see it break, you scummy?"

A hot quarrel sprang up between the two. Mecklin finally stepped between them and ordered them to shut up.

"Mebbe these rains started the foot-log slippin'," he suggested. "Let's get on to camp and eat. Mebbe that'll make us feel better."

In the dead quiet of one o'clock that night, with no rain falling or whisper of breeze blowing, a dead spruce snag thirty feet from their tent suddenly crashed full length to the ground, missing their tent by a scant eight feet. They sprang up, lit the lantern, and looked at the wreckage.

The Mystery of the Ghost Gold 51

"Blasted funny about that tree fallin' down on a still night like this," Mecklin remarked, his voice low and shaky. "Don't look natural-like to me. We've had high wind, and we've had rain, and we've had 'em both together, but that snag stood there solid as a rock!"

Greever jerked out, "We're hoodooed, that's what. They's a hoodoo a-workin' on us. Three times now. . . ."

"Shut up that hoodoo stuff!" Mecklin cut him short. "That sort of talk'll give us all the willywams in mighty short order. This spruce a-fallin' down was just another accident. Go to bed, you big, whiskered baby. What're you shiverin' about? I thought you had some backbone."

They crawled into their blankets again and tried to sleep.

When morning came, and the gray shadows lifted from the spruces, the three ate breakfast and went up the gorge to their diggings. As they cut a channel through the rock debris, one of them was on the lookout all the time, watching for they knew not what.

It happened late that afternoon. They had cut the channel through and gone back to the tunnel, to work inside it. Just before twilight, when they were all three in the tunnel, Mecklin set a tiny powder blast under a stubborn rock. They backed up to the tunnel mouth and awaited the explosion nonchalantly—they had shot off a dozen similar charges.

It was Murph Mecklin again who yelled warning, a second after the little charge went off. In the center of the tunnel a staunch cedar upright, the key prop of their timbering, started skidding to one side at its base. It stopped against a rock, but the roofing timber no longer had solid support. It gave way slowly, writhing like a tortured thing, and the tunnel began caving in. Mecklin leaped outside into the buckbrush, and like a flash Daoust dived after him. But Greever, whose brain was slow as a turtle's, did not entirely escape; his legs and hips were caught by the falling gravel, and he lay pinioned there, yelling and thrashing.

Mecklin pulled him out, and the three of them stood speechless, looking dazedly at the ruined tunnel. Mecklin finally found his tongue.

"If I hadn't seen that upright slippin', we'd be buried alive in that hole. Greever, if you'd left that prop like I fixed it in the first place, 'stead of tamperin'—"

"I didn't tamper!" Greever snarled. "I never touched the thing. I suppose I tampered with that boulder, heh? And that foot-log. And that dead spruce, heh? I tell you we're hoodooed on this job."

Mecklin no longer tried to bolster up his two confederates. He needed bolstering up himself.

As they walked back to the camp they kept close to one another, glancing into the underbrush around them and clutching at their belt-guns when shadows flickered under the dark spruces. A subtle dread was weaving itself around them. The "accidents," one after another, were driving them toward panic.

At camp that evening another blow fell, a blow which could not possibly be set down as accident but had to be

The Mystery of the Ghost Gold 53

interpreted as the work of some hand, whether ghostly or human.

Mecklin was cooking supper, and Daoust was cleaning their tools. Greever had just gone into the tent to stow away a couple of good-sized nuggets he had picked up at the lode. The two men outside heard him bellow suddenly, as if he had been struck a blow, and they leaped into the tent to see what had happened.

Frozen in his tracks, Greever stood holding the can in which they had put their dust and nuggets. "Look't!" he gasped hoarsely, thrusting the can at them. "Look't at what our dust and nuggets have changed into."

Mecklin snatched the can from him and looked. Daoust looked. . . .

The gold dust had changed to yellow sand, the nuggets to bits of heavy, yellow gravel.

For an hour they sat in the darkness of their tent, rifles across their knees, and talked in whispers. It was Mecklin who first got hold of his jumping nerves and could think clearly. Gradually he managed to quiet Greever's panic and the half-breed's superstitious terror.

"Them accidents," he kept saying, "didn't just happen. They was staged. We ought to've seen that. Now this can business proves it. Somebody robbed us, the low-down carcajou. They's somebody around here, a-tryin' to get us and have our lode."

They began laying plans. Courage came back to them with the thought that they were dealing with an enemy of flesh and blood. After eating supper, they put out the fire and lantern and rolled up in their blankets.

Half an hour later Daoust slipped out of his poke, crept noiselessly away from the tent, and faded into the blackness of the spruces. Greever and Mecklin lay listening.

"That 'breed'll get 'em," Greever whispered. "There ain't a white man, 'breed, or Ind'un alive that's his match in a woods. Daoust'll spot the sneaky carcajou out there and give him a knife between the ribs."

But in the gray of morning Daoust slipped back into camp and reported that during his all-night vigil, prowling and circling through the surrounding woods, he had not heard or seen one sign or whisper of an enemy.

"Then we'll go after 'em and hunt 'em down!" Mecklin rasped. "We're bound to strike their trail somewheres, and we'll hang onto it till we run 'em down and stomp 'em into the ground!"

After breakfast they stuck their belts full of cartridges and started combing down the valley, swinging back and forth from rimrock to rimrock, and beating thoroughly through the thick woods. Daoust, ranging ahead, covered the ground like a dog coursing for a cold trail.

They combed the narrow valley to a point eight miles below their camp, and found nothing. The next day they hunted up valley and found no sign of their unknown, shadowy enemy. When they tramped home at nightfall they were morose and quarreling, and their nerves were at the breaking point. Mecklin alone still kept a grip on himself.

Greever snarled at him. "A whoop your hunch was worth! Exceptin' ourselves, there ain't been a live person in this gorge since McPher— I mean, exceptin' ourselves. Daoust would've seen signs. We're hoodooed, Murph Mecklin, I tell you. Hoodooed *and worse!*"

That night, at the same hour that the dead spruce had fallen, Daoust awakened his two partners and bade them listen.

A faraway, hollow noise came echoing down the gorge. It rose high-pitched, died to a whisper, and rose again— weird, mysterious, and hair-raising.

"Wolf," Mecklin grunted, and tried to shrug his shoulders unconcernedly.

"No wolf!" Daoust flatly contradicted.

"Then what might it be, if you know so much?"

" 'Un't know. Never heard animal or bird cry like that."

Greever sat shivering as the call rose and fell in its weird cadence. His teeth chattered; his courage melted into nerveless terror. A whirr of night wings in a thicket made him shudder. A white owl brushing over his head brought him to his feet with an oath.

"That's the cry of a speerit!" he burst out, as the call started again. "Hear it! It's his ghost! McPherson's! He yelled identical like that when I up with the gun and killed—"

Mecklin's hand dropped to his belt and dragged out

his heavy, snub-nosed revolver. "Shut up! You ever open your mouth ag'in about that doin's, you big bawl-baby—just one word about it—and I'll make a ghost of you yourself. That call is some kind of an animal, and the gorge is playin' tricks with the sound, that's all."

The next morning they stayed in camp, haggard and sleepy-eyed. Greever and the 'breed wanted to leave. They were for throwing everything away but their rifles and enough grub to get them out of the Ghost Gold. Mecklin alone kept his nerve. He laughed at their terror, though his laugh was hollow in his own ears. At sunny noonday he drove them up the valley to the Discovery, and set them to hard work to distract their minds.

Twilight came unexpectedly, as a pall of clouds whipped over the mountains and filled the deep valley with shadows. A few heavy drops of rain fell as they threw down their tools and started for camp.

Halfway there Daoust suddenly stopped—his quick ears had caught a noise in the purple spruce shadows up the right-hand slope. As they listened, with bated breath, they heard a sound as of something running—parallel with them.

Greever jerked his rifle to his cheek and fired. With one accord they raced up the slope through the buckbrush in the direction of the noise, shooting again and again into the bushes. The queer sound retreated, came nearer, played with them, led them on and on toward their camp, and then vanished.

They stumbled to the tent and lit the lantern. As the

The Mystery of the Ghost Gold 57

flame rose up and the glow of it widened till it lighted up the nearest trees, Greever pointed suddenly at an object at the edge of the light, a shadow-wrapped object that looked like the head and torso of a man.

Mecklin emptied his belt-gun at it. The object quivered and fell. They went over to it, fearfully, and saw that it was a battered felt hat and coat, riddled with bullet holes.

"Lord A'mighty, it's McPherson's coat and hat!" Greever stammered hoarsely. "He's been here, he has, in the ghost. He's been ha'ntin' us. *He* caused them accidents. Only a speerit could've changed that gold to w'uthless sand!"

From the torn lining of McPherson's coat something white fell out and fluttered to the ground. Mecklin grabbed it up, glanced at it.

"Why—uh," he gulped, his iron nerve deserting him at last, "it's a n-n-note—f-from McPherson."

Greever snatched the note away and stared at it. "Writ in his blood!" he cried brokenly. "Look't—in his own blood! Says we killed him without warnin'. Shot him in the back. And worst of all, we killed him on God A'mighty's Sabbath!"

"It was you killed him!" Daoust cried at Greever. "Let his ha'nt keep 'way from me. I didn't—"

Greever whirled on him. "You was there, too—you was a part of it all—you're as guilty as me—"

"Oh no, we ain't," Mecklin put in. "It was you as shot him, Greever, and it's you he's ha'ntin'. He's a-wantin' your life for his own, and he'll never rest or let us be till you're dead, Greever."

Snarling like an animal in a trap, Greever dragged out his belt-gun. "If you're thinkin' on shootin' me to get rid of his ha'nt, I'll blow your—"

There was a movement at the edge of the fire glow. A man figure stepped out. A cool, level voice said, "*Gentlemen!*"

The three whirled around. Hardly ten steps away a tall, lean man stood looking at them, his rifle level, behind him the half-naked figure of a Blood scout.

"Put your hands up!" the tall man ordered. "Drop that gun, Greever."

For a moment the three were too stupefied to obey. It took them a little time to realize that they were face to face with living men.

"I said, put up your hands!" David Kirke repeated, sharply. "One—two—"

With a yell Charlo Daoust crouched and kicked at the lantern. In wild haste Greever whipped up his gun and shot at David, but he missed by yards in spite of the point-blank range. A bullet from David's rifle smashed into his gun and shattered the weapon to bits. Blindly panicky, Greever whirled to escape, tripped over a chopping block, and fell, but got to his feet, and scrambled into the buckbrush and went fleeing into the black surrounding woods.

The lantern which Daoust had kicked over rolled around on the moss and went out. In the next second

The Mystery of the Ghost Gold

the camp was plunged into darkness. And in the next it was filled with the cries and oaths of a hand-to-hand fight.

David saw Itai-Po leap toward where Daoust had crouched. With a cry of anger at his wrecked plans, he himself sprang forward, swinging a clubbed rifle at the dim form of Mecklin. The stock struck only a glancing blow, and then Mecklin locked with him, clutching his gun hand. They crashed against a tree, and the rifle fell. Locked in a wrestle, they pitched into the buckbrush, hands at each other's throats. They rolled over and over, clutching each other, smashing at each other's face in blind fury. In the darkness they broke loose, sprang to their feet, and grappled; but they tripped over a mat of roots and fell again, still locked together, and started rolling and slipping down the steep hillside.

At the creek edge they brought up against a boulder. David tore free and sprang to his feet. Mecklin scrambled out onto the gravel bar, leaped up, and David closed with him again. In the wan moonlight of the stream bed they smashed at each other. David lunged at Mecklin, wrapped arms around him, picked him up bodily, and slammed him back against the boulder.

It was a jarring, paralyzing fall. Before Mecklin could shake off his daze, David was on top of him, pressing his face down into the gravel and bending his arms behind his back.

A shadow-silent figure moved out upon the gravel bar

toward him. For a second David thought it was the Assiniboin half-breed Daoust, but then he saw that it was Itai-Po, coming to help him with a length of tent-guide rope in his hand.

"What about Daoust, Itai-Po—you put him out?"

The Indian nodded. "I crack'm over head with tent stake plenty. Got him hog-tied hand and foot."

He bent over and began tying Mecklin up.

"Good!" David panted. "See anything more of Greever?"

"No come back," Itai-Po grunted. "Keep on running. You want me track him down?"

David shook his head. "No! We've got our hands full and more, right here. Let him go." He knew that in that wild, forsaken country, without gun or pack or canoe or any human company, Greever had hardly one chance in a thousand of finding his way out alive. He said: "We've got two witnesses, two prisoners to take back with us across the Divide."

7

Near sundown of a brooding September day, a battered canoe nosed in to the landing in the whitewood clump on Bear River. David, Itai-Po, and their prisoners got out and trudged up the path to the Mounted post.

All four of them were weary and travel-worn from the

long fast trip across the Divide. In the last two days and nights they had come a hundred and fifty miles without sleep or rest.

As they passed the Police stables they heard a shout of astonishment, and Constable Dusty Goff came rushing out, a currycomb and brush in his hand, his eyes bulging.

"Great Jumping Jeerusalem!" he gasped. "Where in consternation have you been, sarge? And who's these two mother's sons you've got here, all tied up?"

"Take them up to the butter tub and lock them up safe, Dusty," David said. "See that they get something to eat and a chance to sleep. Itai-Po will answer your questions. I want to report to Inspector Haley."

As he went on to the officer's cabin, he was remembering the deserted Shannon place that he had passed a little while ago, and wondering where Esther and Paul were—if Paul was still alive. The lad had been so weak and sick that August day.

When he knocked at the cabin and went in, Inspector Haley looked at him in amazement—at his torn, muddy clothes, his unshaven face, and the other visible marks of his long, wilderness trip.

"Good Lord!" Haley breathed. "I don't yet know where you've been, Kirke, but it was surely *somewhere*. Sit down. Was it the wild-goose chase you were afraid it might be?"

"I was lucky and I did all I set out to do," David said.

"I cleared up the McPherson murder and brought back two of the three killers."

Briefly he told the story of his and Itai-Po's patrol across the Rockies and into the uncharted Ghost Gold. Of his original suspicions. Of the trip across and Sockeye Sullivan. Of the lode and the three murderers he'd found there, working it without the slightest fear that the long arm of the Mounted would reach across a thousand miles of mountainous wilderness and bring them to justice for their murder.

"That's about all, sir," he finished. "Sullivan is in charge of that lode. If we can locate any of McPherson's people, Sullivan will get a quarter and they the rest. Otherwise he can file for himself. Legally, the gold that McPherson left with the Shannons belongs to them; he said it was to be theirs if he didn't happen to come back. It can be sent to them now, since their innocence and their testimony have been proved."

Inspector Haley drew a deep breath. "It's all an astounding story, Kirke. As remarkable a patrol as the Force ever turned in. I'll get off my report to headquarters at once." He was silent a moment, thrumming on the desk. "As for the gold that McPherson left with the Shannons, we won't have to send it to them. Just after you went away, Paul came down sick, and I had him brought in here to the post, where Dr. Whittier could look after him. He seems to be picking up a bit, but it's still touch and go."

The Mystery of the Ghost Gold

David started a little. "You mean that Esther—then she—is she here?"

"Yes. We fixed up one of the *métis* cabins for them." He looked at David thoughtfully for a long moment. "I think I understand this whole sorry business, Kirke, except for one point. You say that all along you suspected that some bush-sneak gentry killed McPherson for his map. Why, then, did you have the Shannons arrested and brought to trial?"

"For their own safety, sir," David answered. "You know that everybody considered their story flimsy. Feeling against them was running pretty high and it got so ugly that I had to do something. There's always an element that wants to take things into their own hands. I had to guard the Shannon cabin every night for a week. It seemed to me that an open arrest, trial, and acquittal was the only way to head off something very dreadful."

"But why didn't you tell Esther this?"

"Before the trial she had troubles enough, sir, without my letting her know that on two different nights I stopped parties that were going to 'visit' her and Paul. And after the trial she was so bitter that she wouldn't listen."

Haley thrummed on the desk. Finally he said, "I think I'll go down and talk to Esther, Kirke. This story will lift a heavy load from her and Paul. I'm going to tell her myself all that you've told me. I don't think you're very good at tooting your own horn. I'm sure she'll want to see you and thank you. If you'll stay here, I'll send her up."

David objected hastily, "Good heavens—not now, sir. Look how I look. I want to shave and dress. . . ."

"That's something else you don't know about women," Haley remarked. "She's not interested in you as a fancy Dan. For her sake you went through two thousand miles of hardship and danger, and that's how you look, and that's how she ought to see you."

From the cabin window David watched the inspector cross the Police quadrangle and knock at one of the *métis* cabins by the freight-wagon trail. He was fagged out and sleepless but he forgot all that as he watched the cabin where Haley had gone. The slow minutes of his waiting seemed endless. He was shaken with the uncertainty and suspense, and when he saw Esther come out at last, he left the cabin and went across to meet her.

Far away westward the sun was just inching down behind the massive ranges, and a sharp evening chill was creeping into the air. In the scattered clouds overhead the long, strange shadows of the Rockies were shifting and weaving, like a slow panorama of the Western Prairies.

When he met Esther on the path beyond the barracks, she stood stock-still and looked at him, her brown eyes seeing and understanding the signs of the long patrol that he had made for her sake. Presently she laid her hand on his arm and said, "Can you forgive me, David?"

He gulped a little at that and scuffed awkwardly at the

gravel. "It was—uh—pretty bad for everybody concerned, but it's all past," he managed. The afterglow of the sun was tangled in her hair. He drew her arm through his and said, "Let's walk a little. There's so much I've got to tell you, Esther. It couldn't be said before, but I can say it now—if you'll listen."

Mannikin Talk

Under Katahka's deft fingers, the mannikin began to tell a story.

*I*N THE SWIRLING twilight of an Arctic storm, Sergeant Glenmawr and his four-dog team reached the winter camp of the Pikliermiut and halted in the middle of the circle of igloos.

Wary and uneasy, the Mounted sergeant glanced around sharply through the flying spindrift, realizing that the Eskimo band numbered twenty hunters—against his lone self. He saw no one abroad, and knew the Pikliermiut were sleeping out the blizzard in the Eskimo fashion. After getting his rifle from the sled and freeing his holster gun, he called out, "*Aksunai*, Pikliermiut! I come as friend."

As he waited, he looked around at the snow-block igloos and the big *kozgee* or council house, made of caribou skins and banked high with warm drift. About the whole place there was not one sign of white-man ways. The remote, primitive hunting camp, located on the blizzard-swept beach within easy reach of the seal holes, seemed to him like a page out of man's Stone Age.

Awakened by his shout, the Pikliermiut came pouring

out of their snowhouses and surrounded him. The barking of their dogs, the soft *"Aah-ee's"* of curiosity from the round-faced women, and the guttural grunts of the stocky men made a noisy greeting. Aware that his mission and maybe his very life depended on how they received him, Glenmawr studied the dark, broad faces around his sled, and intuitively he sensed how things stood:

The band knew why he'd come, all right. They knew and they were on guard against him, down to the smallest *illillegah* and the last husky. They did not seem particularly hostile, at least not yet. From the covert winks and grins of the hunters at one another he saw they were confident that they could stymie him, as they had already stymied Corporal Redfern that first time and the inspector's party that second time.

"I'll be double-dimmied if you do!" Glenmawr thought; and he swore by all the ancient gods of far-off Wales that he was going to nail this Mugwa fellow, by hook or crook, and on top of that he was going to teach these Pikliermiut a lesson they would not soon forget.

After he had ceremoniously exchanged *"Aksunai"* with every one of the twenty-two men—in the fifty-below-zero storm—they made him welcome, with the friendliness that comes natural to Innuit peoples. Two of the hunters untoggled the bow lines of his huskies, and others brought frozen tomcod for the team. Willing hands grabbed the sled and whisked it inside the *kozgee*. As for Sergeant Glenmawr himself. . . .

A hunter led the Yellow-striped *kabluna* into his igloo

and tendered him a heaped-up bowl of seal beef. Then Glenmawr was invited into the next igloo and ate oil-soaked fish. In the third he was given huge slices of the sharp-tasty stomach contents of a caribou that had moss-fed. . . . From snowhouse to snowhouse the *kabluna* progressed, crawling over the dogs that lay in the warm tunnel entrances, and stared at by the bug-eyed little *ill-illegahs* up on the sleeping platforms, till he had heroically eaten his way around the entire village and was back at the *kozgee* again.

When he went into the council house he found the Pikliermiut men waiting for him, sitting around the *kozgee* wall, their faces dimly lit by the guttering seal-oil lamps. Glenmawr walked across to his sled and sat down. A hush fell, except for the muffled rip and howl of the storm outside.

"Last year in the Moon-of-the-Blue-Goose-Nesting," he began, speaking the Innuit tongue without halt, "your small neighbor band, the Oklogmiut, were wiped out by the fever sickness. Only two hunters of the Oklogmiut survived. They came here with their wives and *illillegahs* and asked to live henceforth with the Pikliermiut, and you allowed them to stay. They built their igloos by the side of your own; they joined with you in the seal hunting and the caribou spearing-surround. Then in the Moon-of-Flying-Hoarfrost one of your men, this Mugwa, quarreled with a hunter and flung a spear through him, so that the Oklogmiut man died— Is not all this true, O Pikliermiut?"

The men slowly nodded. Sergeant Glenmawr filled his pipe with *stemmo* and went on. "Word of this killing drifted out to the white man's fort on the River-of-a-Hundred-Mouths. One of the Yellow-striped *kablunas* there traveled over here to arrest Mugwa and take him to the fort. But Mugwa could not be found. Later came three Yellow-Stripes looking for him, but again Mugwa was not here—neither in the village or at the seal holes or the caribou yards. Nor would any man of the Pikliermiut tell the Yellow-Stripes where Mugwa had hidden himself."

The chief hunter gazed at the sergeant steadily and said, "It is not the way of the Pikliermiut, O *Kabluna*, to deliver a blood brother into the hands of strangers. Our quarrels are our quarrels and no concern of the Yellow-striped-horsemen-without-horses."

Glenmawr stared back at the hunter. "Your words are like the chatter of the foolish *wheeskeejaun* bird. It is our concern that all the tribes of this country live at peace with one another, and that all the men within a tribe keep the peace with one another. When the Goat-Eater Indians tried that time to steal your women at your summertime lodges, while the hunters were gone, we sent men with guns and halted them. If your igloos should become empty in the Moon-of-the-Lean-Wolves-Wailing, we would send you a sledload of food. Therefore your troubles are our troubles, and your quarrels are our quarrels. Therefore when a man among you kills another without reason, it is indeed our concern. This Mugwa, this flinger-of-spears-at-men, must be punished. You must tell me where he is hiding."

The sergeant paused. The sidelong glances of the Pikliermiut hunters at one another told him what he already knew—the killer was hidden somewhere not far from the village, and the whole band was protecting him. With an isolated tribe like these Pikliermiut the blood tie was all-powerful. It overrode their fear of the law, their sense of justice, and even their own secret wish to be rid of a bully like this Mugwa.

Undoubtedly, Glenmawr reflected, the killer was holed up in the hills that lay just inland from the village. Undoubtedly the Pikliermiut were taking him food and seal oil so that he would not have to stir out of his cave when the Mounted parties came.

The chief hunter asked blandly, "And what if we do not choose to tell you, O *Kabluna*, where Mugwa is hiding?"

The sergeant snapped back, "Then I will make magic and find him myself! I will go out into the storm and summon my Familiars, and they will whisper to me of Mugwa's whereabouts."

The chief hunter grinned at him. "Our magic is stronger than your magic, O *Kabluna*." He pointed at the old tribal shaman. "Old Neegeetonga will beat on his *sowyunga* and drive your Familiars away, as he did when the other *kablunas* came."

"Maybe!" Glenmawr grunted. "We will see."

Casually he looked around the circle of swarthy faces

to locate the man he wanted to talk to—the man whose help he was confident of getting. Katahka, the hunter was called. He was the remaining one of those two Oklogmiut whose tiny band had been wiped out and who had joined these Pikliermiut. After the killing, Katahka had taken the murdered man's wife and *illillegahs* into his own igloo; but the tribal blood-law had kept him, an outsider, from retaliating at Mugwa for the wanton slaying.

This Katahka, the sergeant had figured, would surely want to see his tribe-brother avenged. If given the slightest chance, the man would tip the Police off to Mugwa's hiding place. "This blood-code business works both ways," Glenmawr had argued with the Officer Commanding, at the fort. "This Katahka won't rest, can't rest, till he puts a spear through Mugwa or sees him dangling from a noose. I'll bet my watch against a gallus button that Katahka will help us out."

It was this conviction that had brought him on the three-hundred-mile trip in the dead of Arctic winter.

Remembering Corporal Redfern's description, he spotted Katahka easily enough—a round-faced hunter of middle age, with several livid weals across his left cheek where a white bear once had clawed him. The man was sitting against the far wall of the *kozgee,* and Glenmawr realized that the Pikliermiut did not trust Katahka and were keeping him away from the white man. He remembered, now, that he had not been taken into Katahka's igloo or been given any chance to talk to the hunter.

"Darn it all," he thought, and a little of his confidence drained away, "it's not going to be easy to get in a private word with him, when everybody's watching him and me like hawks. If they catch us talking, they'll slit his throat with a walrus knife."

Taking care not to appear interested, he sized Katahka up, and the conviction grew on him that the hunter not only wouldn't be given a chance to help him but didn't want to. A round-faced, round-headed fellow, the man looked much too amiable and stolid to harbor any vengeance. In fact he was paying less attention to the *kabluna* than the other hunters were. He had fashioned himself a *beetinka* plaything, a small, seal-gut mannikin such as the hunters sometimes amused themselves with during their long waits at the seal holes; and with a foolish smile on his face he was manipulating the toy by its sinew threads. Engrossed in the *beetinka's* antics, he seemed utterly oblivious to the council talk.

Glenmawr swore at him silently. "You dumb slug! Here I foot-slog three hundred miles through an Arctic woolly-whipper, expecting help from you, and you sit there fiddling with that silly doo-dad!"

His hopes for any aid from Katahka went slumping down to zero. For a little while he smoked in glum silence, cudgeling his brains for a way to locate the elusive Mugwa.

To hunt for the man back in that jumble of frozen hills, cliffs, and willow lakes was as useless as searching for a raindrop that had fallen into the sea. Corporal Redfern had spent a month combing those hills. The corporal had tried also to trail the Pikliermiut men who took food to Mugwa, but they had made the trip only during blizzards that whipped their tracks shut instantly.

And all the arguments, pleas, and threats that Inspector Greyson and his party could think up had shattered against that code of the blood tie.

The wall of silence all around him angered Glenmawr. As he glared across at Katahka and the seal-gut mannikin, he thought savagely, "I could choke you. What a washout—"

A sudden jolt went through him as he noticed the antics of the grotesquely lifelike *beetinka*. For a second or two he could only stare at the toy and the foolish, smiling Katahka.

"Great Jeerusalem! Look what that fellow's been trying to do. And I didn't catch on. *I'm* the dumb slug—or maybe it was getting stuffed with all that grub."

He made himself look away from Katahka for a minute or two. A chill little fear crept through him lest any of the other men should get suspicious and watch that *beetinka*. If they caught on, they would pin Katahka to the wall with half a dozen spears.

To draw their attention to himself, he swung the talk away from Mugwa and began telling stories about the country of the white man, down in the Lands of the Sun. From years of experience with remote Innuit bands he knew that the simplest little story about that country was a fairy tale to them; and he started telling them about his last furlough trip—his trip back to old Wales to marry the girl who had waited there for him, and bring her back with him to the Canadian North.

"On this journey of mine," he recounted, "at the igloo place called Edmonton, I got on the great long sled that runs on tracks of iron instead of ice. And the creature that pulls this sled is bigger than twenty water bears, and eats black rocks, and in one day's time it hauls the huge sled farther than a swift Innuit hunter can travel in a moon."

The Pikliermiut all were leaning forward, their eyes fixed on him; and Glenmawr went on, "And at the igloo place called Winnipeg I got into a great canoe that has wings and flies through the air; and in the space of a day it carried me across mountains and lakes and tundra and rivers to the Eastern Sea. And there a great *oomiak*, big as an iceberg, carried me across this sea to a huge igloo place called London, where the *kablunas* are like ants for numbers and have tunnels underground like ants, and the igloos are as big as hills. . . ."

Without breaking the flow of his story or letting the eyes of the hunters wander from him, he looked casually again at Katahka and the *beetinka*. Under the Eskimo's deft fingers the mannikin had been tumbling, dancing, wrestling; it had imitated animals, stalked seals, and pantomimed the age-old legends of the Innuits. But as Katahka caught the sergeant's eye on him, the *beetinka* began telling a little story of a trip. . . .

Yawning and stretching, the mannikin got up from

sleep and started eastward, shielding its eyes from the morning sun. It came to a river and there turned right, back into the frozen hills. Watching intently, Glenmawr counted three river bends and a fork. There the mannikin turned right again and came to the foot of a high cliff. Then it bent low, like a person creeping through a low cave mouth, stopped, and lay down to sleep.

The sergeant went on smoothly with his own story—of old Wales, and Gwenda and their honeymoon trip back to Canada; but his blood was pounding. "The river fork, the cliff, the first cave—I couldn't miss. Not bad, Katahka, and your doodad—right under the noses of twenty-two men!"

It was late the next afternoon, in the taut, still cold of sixty below zero, when Glenmawr once again halted his dogs in the center of the igloo circle. He was weary and hungry, and he ached to think of the long white leagues back to the fort and to Gwenda. But he would be going back triumphant. He had a prisoner trussed up in the sleeping bag on his sled, and the prisoner was the sullen-eyed Mugwa.

He had brought his prisoner back there deliberately, to show the Pikliermiut that one Yellow-Stripe was unafraid of a whole village; that he walked with the power and might of an unseen host. And he had been worrying about Katahka and wanted to forestall any danger to him. If the Pikliermiut should ever become suspicious of Katahka, the amiable roundhead would get speared and stuck down through a seal hole.

In an awed silence the Pikliermiut, standing close around the sled, looked at the scowling Mugwa and then at the rock-faced sergeant. Ruefully the chief hunter observed, "Your magic is in truth greater than our magic, O *Kabluna*. Since you left us yesterday, old Neegeetonga has not ceased beating his *sowyunga*. But it was useless."

"You have learned wisdom," the sergeant remarked. "It is always useless to stand against the Yellow-Stripes. I can understand that Mugwa was of your blood, but nevertheless you must never again shield a killer—"

He caught sight of Katahka, back at the edge of the crowd. The hunter was still carrying the *beetinka* and seemed completely indifferent toward the prisoner on the sled; but Glenmawr noticed that his eyes were going uneasily from face to face around him.

The sergeant called out at him accusingly, "But you, Katahka, who would not help the other Yellow-Stripes or help me—you I cannot understand. You are of the murdered man's own blood; you have his woman and *ill-illegahs* in your very igloo, and yet you would not tell me one word or lift one finger to avenge your blood brother! You are a worm, O Katahka! A worm, a rabbit, a thing of the mud! Get out of my sight! Go and fiddle with the silly doodad!"

Very meekly Katahka bowed his head, under the lash of the white man's tongue. But as he turned away he caught the sergeant's eyes and made a slight gesture toward the *beetinka* in his hand. Sergeant Glenmawr looked, looked twice, and had to swipe a mitten across his mouth to hide his laugh.

The mannikin in Katahka's hand was dangling prophetically in the air, with one of the sinew threads noosed around its neck.

A Relic of the Vikings

Ogohko roared with laughter. "Now wasn't that old story a whopper?" he demanded.

*I*N THE LASHING fury of the Arctic storm, Sergeant Imley and his young Eskimo guide were cutting snow blocks and building a small igloo—pitching their camp, in the fashion of wise hunters, on the spot where they had made their game kill.

Just a few minutes ago the young Ogohko, breaking trail, had shot point-blank at a dim wraith in the storm and brought down a white yearling caribou.

All day the Mounted sergeant and Ogohko, in the teeth of the polar blizzard, had pushed north across the ice sierras of Fox Land, so near the top of the world that from longitude to longitude was only a fair day's travel. Though the woolly-whipper was so blinding that they could hardly see twenty paces into the queer half-light, the stalwart young Eskimo guide had followed unerringly the age-old *komatik* trail that wound northward through the frozen coastal hills.

It was good to be out exploring again, Sergeant Imley mused, catching the snow blocks that Ogohko cut and tossed at him. And good to be a hundred long miles from the tiny Mounted post where he and Constable Stuart had been stationed for two endless years, apparently forgotten by the Force and by all the rest of humanity down in the Lands of the Sun. To keep themselves from "shaking hands with the willows," he had encouraged Stuart to prospect for placer gold in the moraine gravels of the mountains, while he himself had begun exploring into a mystery that was a thousand years old and as baffling as it was ancient.

He was hunting for proof that the Icelander Vikings of ten centuries ago had discovered Fox Land during their far sea-wanderings, as the Sagas stated. Under the boldest of the Viking captains, they had planted a colony on the Arctic island and built their stone summer huts there and had fought with the native Innuits—so the Sagas ran.

But in two years of hunting, the sergeant had not found one stone of those ancient *hellu-hutta* nor one faintest evidence that the tall Sea Warriors had ever set foot on that remote polar shore.

He capped the little beehive igloo with a block of snow and then crawled in at the tunnel entrance, with his tump pack and eider sleeping-poke. Above the savage fury of the blizzard outside he could hear big Ogohko singing lustily while flensing the caribou. After a long succession of stolid and silent guides, the buoyant Ogohko seemed to him a rare find as a trail companion. A member of the Iglulermiut band, which dwelt near the Mounted post, the high-spirited young Innuit had

A *Relic of the Vikings*

been keen for the month-long trip, even though he was only recently married to the sunny, roundfaced girl called Aikalwa. On the trail he was always singing, laughing—at the slightest pretext for merriment he would throw back his head and roar softly.

More important still in Sergeant Imley's eyes, Ogohko was a treasure trove of Eskimo legend and superstition. He seemed to know more tales of the snowlands than the oldest shamans, and he told them with huge gusto, although he himself believed not one word of them. A born iconoclast, he was derisive toward the shaman magic and folklore of his people. He would finish a story with a great flourish and then demand, "Now isn't that a whopper?" and then he would toss his head and roar till the fox tail on the parka danced and jiggered.

Presently Ogohko came crawling in. The sergeant cooked thick caribou collops on the primus plate and made scones, and they ate. After they had put out the primus and lighted the seal-oil lamp, they leaned back on their pokes.

"This stretch of shore," the sergeant said, in the Innuit tongue, "is the last I have left to hunt, Ogohko. The storm has swept the beach plain bare of snow. Bare enough that the old stone huts will show, if there be any along this coast."

"Stone by stone," Ogohko remarked, "I will eat whatever old stone huts you will find, O *Kabluna*." And he tossed his head and laughed.

In the dim yellow light Sergeant Imley studied the

big youngster. Somehow Ogohko seemed different from his fellow-Iglulermiut; different indeed from all the Innuits of the great Arctic island. He tried to pin this strangeness down and word it, but he could not, and he told himself it was only his imagination. He knew that under the flash and play of the Borealis, in the long winter dark, a man's eyes sometimes did odd tricks with him. In the queer gloom he had shot at an Arctic lemming on a windrow ten feet away in the belief that it was a polar bear loping along a ridge-line; and he had seen hunters drop their spears and flee in terror from a snowshoe rabbit. So Ogohko's strangeness, he thought, was likely a mere fancy.

"Now that we have made a meat kill, Ogohko," he said, "we can camp here for seven sleeps and hunt this coast."

"In seven-and-seventy sleeps you will find no stone huts, *Kabluna.*"

"But your own people have legends about the Sea Men, Ogohko."

"Those stories are old wives' tales!"

"Maybe," Imley twitted him, "you are trying to dishearten me so that you can get back the sooner to Aikalwa. Ah, that is it. She is very pretty, your girl-wife. I do not blame you, Ogohko, for wishing to go home. But we came here to hunt for the *hellu-hutta.* Soon enough you will be with Aikalwa again."

Ogohko tossed his head and laughed softly. "I will hunt with you till your legs wear off, O Yellow-striped-

A Relic of the Vikings

horseman-without-a-horse. We will comb the sea edge and the beaches and the hills here till your tongue drags on the snow. I will be your guide to Nudujen Inlet, to Tunniren, Tudjan, and even to Akpansoak. But we will find no stone houses."

The sergeant jerked a little with surprise. Ogohko had named the exact path of that long-ago Viking band in its legendary wandering! The exact path that the Sagas had set down. How under heaven had he known? Or was it merely coincidence?

"Do you not, Ogohko," he prompted, "believe one word of those legends about the Sea Warriors?"

"Not one breath!" Ogohko said stoutly. "And more, *Kabluna*—even if they were true, you would find no stone houses. True or false, no houses."

"You must have some story to explain that," Imley said. He handed over his tin of *stemmo* for Ogohko's pipe. "What is it?"

"It is a story," Ogohko replied, helping himself generously, "that was told to me by old Natagliak, who bleeds at the mouth when he talks; to him it was told by Eumenek, his father; to him by Tojak; to him by Kriliak; to him by—"

"Stop!" Imley interposed. "My ears buzz with names of the long-dead. How many have been the generations?"

Ogohko held up a hand. "Four times that. And the first teller in that long ago was Knuluk, chief hunter of the Iglulermiut, who could take two bears by the scruff of their necks and bang their heads together."

"That," Imley remarked, "really is a whopper. But what has that to do with the legend of the Sea Warriors?"

"Nothing, O Yellow-striped-horseman-without-a-horse —except that both lies came from the same mouth!" The young giant roared softly and tossed his head at having scored so decisively.

After a moment Imley said, "Tell me about this Knuluk of twenty generations ago, who played so roughly with polar bears."

Ogohko stuffed his pipe with still more of the sergeant's precious, dwindling *stemmo*, and finally began recounting.

It was very, very long ago, O *Kabluna*. As many generations ago as I have fingers and toes—plus one to make up for the toe that is frozen off. In that long ago the Iglulermiut were the strongest of the Island tribes, numbering five times as many igloos as now.

One day in the Moon-of-Birds-Flying-Southward, a hunter from a tribe far up the coast came stumbling into the village of the Iglulermiut. He was bleeding from a dozen great wounds, and one arm was cloven off at the shoulder; but before he dropped dead he told of what had happened to him and his tribe, the Yakakapmiut.

He told of how a strange great *oomiak* had been storm-driven ashore and wrecked, along the coast to the north. Of how sixty giant strangers, who were fair of face and sang as they marched, had come ashore with their wives

A Relic of the Vikings

and *illillegahs*. The men wore shirts of iron, he said, and headpieces of iron, and they swung axes of iron behind round shields of oxhide.

All the hunters of the Yakakapmiut went out to meet them. The strangers asked for peace, but the Yakakapmiut gave them a shower of arrows and harpoons instead, and the battle was begun.

It was long and bloody, O *Kabluna*, there on the ice plain by Tudjan. The Yakakapmiut slew many of the strangers, but every giant that fell was ringed around with the bodies of hunters who would hunt no more. And at last the singing Sea Men stood alone on the battle ice, cleansing their weapons and looking around at the Yakakapmiut dead. Only the hunter whose arm was cloven from the shoulder by the stroke of an ax escaped the slaughter and fled to warn the Iglulermiut.

On hearing the news, Knuluk gathered his men and gave orders. The women and *illillegahs* were taken on *komatiks* to a place of safety in a hidden ice gorge. Harpoons were piled handily, spearheads were removed, and knives were whetted against green walrus ivory. Hunters and weapons were all in readiness when the fair-faced giants, singing and stroking iron on iron, appeared in the valley and came down to meet the Iglulermiut.

At their singing the hunters trembled, but they were brave men and they moved forward with Knuluk to confront the enemy.

After the great fight with the Yakakapmiut there were but thirty of the giants, and many of them bore wounds of arrow or harpoon. But they came on, neither faster nor slower, and approached the Iglulermiut, and at their head strode a giant, taller than any of them, tossing his ax in the air and catching it.

When they were still two long harpoon-flings away, this leader of the singing strangers grasped an iron-shod spear, drew back his arm, and hurled the weapon as never before had an Eskimo seen a spear hurled. It sailed over Knuluk's head and over all his band of men and shattered upon the ice beyond. Whereupon the leader raised his hand and the singing and stroking of iron on iron stopped.

"*Aksunai!*" he shouted, so that the hills around flung back his voice. "*Aksunai*, Eskimos, we come peacefully. Be wise and let us pass."

The Iglulermiut laughed in scorn, and Knuluk called back, "Peacefully, O White Skins? Your wounds are still green from the slaughter of the Yakakapmiut."

"It is no fault of ours if our trail be red with blood," answered the leader. "We sought no battle; it was forced upon us. We want only to pass your village peacefully and avoid bloodshed. Our sea-canoe was storm-cast upon these shores, and we are jetsam. We would get back to our people, and our trail is long and weary. If we are to meet those of our own blood again, we must travel south a hundred sleeps to Helluland, of the Flat Stones. Perhaps we must travel south even two hundred sleeps, to the shores called Vinland, where Leif the Lucky and

A Relic of the Vikings

Njal the One-Eye visit in summer. Therefore bid your skraelings move aside and let us pass."

Knuluk, being wise, would have agreed to the request. But the Iglulermiut began crying out, "They slaughtered our kinsmen, the Yakakapmiut! Even so will they deal with us."

A knot of young hunters ran forward and flung their weapons. The tall leader caught a spear in mid-air and tossed it through an Eskimo. The fair-haired women of the giants fell back; the singing and stroking of iron on iron began afresh; the Iglulermiut surged forward, and the battle with the Sea Men was on.

Their shields of oxhide made a solid wall, *Kabluna*, against which the Eskimo harpoons and spears rattled harmlessly. A shower of iron-tipped arrows cut down half a score of the Iglulermiut, for they knew nothing of fighting in a body. Hence, when the shield-wall of the tall warriors struck them they could not hold ground, though they were as five to one. With their iron axes and with never an abatement in their singing, the strangers cut a broad path through the huddled Eskimos.

Knuluk and a dozen picked men flung themselves forward to break the shield-wall, but they were tossed back like spindrift from a cliff. The numbers that were slain were five of the wounded strangers and thirty of the Iglulermiut.

A knot of ten Eskimos ran up the hillslope and tossed harpoons into the midst of the enemy. Five of the fair-faces marched up the hill and slew the ten hunters.

Before they could return through the deep snow they were hemmed in by Knuluk's men. Still singing, as they plied spear and battle-ax, they fell forward on their faces, one by one. The numbers of the slain were twelve of the giants and fifty of the hunters.

Knuluk then sent men to make a show of attacking the fair-faced women, but these fought like fierce she-bears and drew bow with deadly aim. When the warriors saw their women attacked, they fell back orderly, still singing and stroking iron on iron, to form a wall about their wives and *illillegahs*, as the bulls of the musk oxen do against wolf packs.

Craftily Knuluk drew his men off. They were sick of the senseless slaughter they had brought upon themselves, but the peace they had refused could no more be brought back than the slain could rise and walk. It was battle to the death now.

"See, we have killed many of them," Knuluk encouraged his fighters. "Those that remain have no more of the iron-tipped spears. They are flinging back at us only the weapons that we throw at them. Let us fight from a little distance, so that they will have to use their bows. When they have no more arrows, then we will close with them and avenge our brethren speedily."

But the strangers were quick to see through this stratagem and they ceased shooting. Their bows, *Kabluna*, were as tall as they, and so strong that not an Eskimo could draw an arrow to the head. The strings were of the flaxen hair of the fair-faced women; and when a bow-

A Relic of the Vikings

string broke, a woman sprang up ready with a new string braided from her own hair. Ah, they were fighting fiends, *Kabluna*. Their very singing, which rose and fell with the tide of battle, chilled the hearts of the Iglulermiut.

When Knuluk saw that they had guessed his cunning, he bade part of his men hurry to the igloos and fetch all the hides of caribou and walrus they could find. Then he ordered big shields fashioned of the hides; big enough that behind each a dozen men could hide in safety. The fair-faced warriors loosed a shower of arrows while the shields were in the making, but Knuluk merely drew his men back out of range. Four of the great shields were made and placed properly on the four sides of the enemy. Then Knuluk gave a shout, and the ramparts moved forward.

Still the giants sang and stroked iron on iron, even those who knelt bleeding in the snow, while the tall leader tossed his ax in the air and caught it.

Behind their shelters of hides the Iglulermiut moved steadily forward, certain that now they could break the shield-wall and come at the warriors body to body. The fair-faces arched arrows high into the air and wounded several Eskimos, but so many of the hunters had died that those who lived had grown dull toward death and had little fear of it.

The arrows ceased. No spears were tossed from either side. Even the singing quavered as the great shields moved forward foot by foot and met the circle of warriors. Massed behind their shelters, the Iglulermiut struck irresistibly. The circle was broken, and the hunters leaped into the midst.

It was battle-ax against spear; one warrior against four hunters. In that fierce melee the Eskimos fought silently with their long knives; the fair-faces slashed and hewed with short, heavy swords. They could cleave a man's brainpan at one stroke, and they fought like bull bears at the spearing-surround.

But they had been flung apart; they no longer stood leg to leg and shield to shield. Moreover the Iglulermiut had learned to strike them where the iron shirt met the iron headdress—where the neck could be pierced. The tall warriors were battling fiends, sinking to a knee under a thrust but rising to cleave an Eskimo's head from his shoulder even while they struggled in the death throe. But as wolves can bring down the male of the caribou, so the remnant of Iglulermiut, fighting silently, brought down the warriors one by one, till only the tall leader was still on his feet, battling.

Knuluk and five others were thrusting at him, and his iron shirt ran red with his own blood. He swung his heavy ax in a circle by the chain which held it to his wrist, and brained two hunters who had flung themselves at him. While he swung his ax, he drew his hand across his eyes to wipe away the blood so that he might see clearly. Even Knuluk trembled at the ferocity of his face.

In the breathing space that they gave him, he turned and saw that all his warriors were lying on the snow. With a great voice he called an order to the fair-haired women, who thereupon began to seize weapons and turn them against themselves. But at a word from Knuluk, the Iglulermiut ran in and tore the weapons from the women's hands.

The tall leader did not see this. Bearing the song of the warriors by himself, he sprang at the knot of hunters around Knuluk. A spear thrust broke the fastening of his iron headdress, and he fought uncovered. He dashed his ax against the face of an Eskimo, and with a backstroke he clove through the shoulder of Knuluk, so that the great hunter thereafter was helpless as a babe.

But then a spear from the hand of Knuluk's son hurtled through the air, and it struck the tall leader in the throat. He sank to a knee, sank to the snow. . . . His song, and the slaughter, and the trek of the wandering, fair-faced giants were ended.

By the order of Knuluk, the flaxen-haired women were spared. "They are of the blood of the great warriors," he said. "We will take them to wife among us, and thereafter the blood of the fighting Sea Men will run in the veins of the Iglulermiut."

Sergeant Imley sat silent, still hearing the din and echoes of that ancient, greathearted battle. As he stared into the guttering seal-oil flame, he felt that the story he had just heard was as wild and stark as any told by the Sagas themselves. As wild and fierce as the epics of Leif and Eric and the Njal who was burned under the oxhide.

Presently a chuckle from Ogohko brought him back to

the present. The young Eskimo was looking at him and laughing.

"Now wasn't that old story a whopper?" he demanded, with a toss of the parka foxtail. "Ho! Singing giants dressed in iron. And women braiding bowstrings of their flaxen hair! And later bearing children to the hunters of my people, the Iglulermiut! The tale of Knuluk cracking bear heads together is as nothing, *Kabluna*, to that whopper."

As the sergeant looked at Ogohko, in the yellow light glow, he gasped in astonishment. As by a lightning flash he suddenly realized what was strange about the stalwart young Innuit. The blue-gray eyes, the old-Norse face, the hair with a touch of flaxen— Heaven and Valhalla, there was Viking blood in the veins of this strapping young Eskimo guide! The blood of those old Seafarers, ten centuries dead!

"Is it not a most silly story, O *Kabluna?*" Ogohko insisted, laughing softly.

Imley got hold of himself. "Quite silly," he agreed, meeting those gray-blue eyes. "Laugh a big laugh at it, Ogohko—it is truly one whopper of a story."

Shepherd of the Storm

Gabriel's long, bone-smashing right landed on the tilted jaw.

*T*HE ROARING SASKATCHEWAN blizzard slammed open the door of the Mounted barracks and blew in six feet of sandy-whiskered, ice-sheathed corporal. While he fumbled to find the doorknob, he drew a hand from his bearskin glove and clawed at the sleet in his eyelashes.

"Shut the doo-or, Zy!" Constable Coffey yelped, from his perch on top a double-decker bunk. It was considerably warmer up there.

"—the do-oo-or, Zy!" chorused three other constables and Sergeant Pedneault, who were playing euchre behind the red-hot stove.

The six men, along with Inspector Nuttall, were the entire detachment at that Police post in western Saskatchewan. The Klondike rush, then in its full swing, had drawn heavily on the whole North-West Mounted. The little gang of hard-bitten veterans under Nuttall had to police a park-prairie region as big as a state; had to take care of the immigrants trekking across from Winnipeg, and send monthly patrols north and east to keep check on the Strong-Woods Crees; and they carried on an endless battle with the Border rings of smugglers and branding-iron artists who kept springing up like toadstools.

In a voice that resembled a buffalo cough, Corporal Zsbyski rapped, "How the dimmity did you expect me to get in—down the chimley, like Santy Claus? Or did you expect me to stay out in the stable?"

His jacket crackled as he pulled it off. For a minute it stood grotesquely stiff in front of the stove; then it slowly began to wilt.

"You should've come in off patrol when this woolly-whipper first struck, Zy," Sergeant Pedneault remarked. "The rest of us all got back in by ten o'clock this morning. What I mean, this blizzard is dangerous. Nuttall gave orders that nobody sticks his nose outside till it stops. When the weather holds off till near Christmas, like this fall, the first woolly-whipper is always a honey-peloozer, they say. Even so, this beats any blizzard I ever saw. It's so cold you can spit icicles, except it's so cold you can't spit."

"Yeah, our nice weather sure ended abrupt," Constable Hightower put in. "Last night I slept in one blanket on the open prairie, and it was still balmy at eight this morning. Then a little rain, a little sleet, and then—stop kicking me, Breden, I know what to lead—then, bang! she came whooping over the hills and dropped the tempeechur ten feet below freezo before I could aim my hoss for the post and git going."

"Zy's stiff coat there 'minds me," Breden commented, "that my jacket got wet this morning in that sleety rain,

Shepherd of the Storm

so I took it off, and carried it on the saddle. The first howl struck so quick that the coat froze bone-hard before I could get it on."

"It handled me rougher than anybody," said Constable Morrow, the sergeant's partner, "because I was ankling across Muskeg Bottoms where she got a clean swat at me. She'd hit me one way and knock me over, then hit me the other and knock me back. I'd be leaning ag'inst her, and she'd stop so sudden I'd fall down. Finally I got a smart idee and I stretched my coattails out wide for a sail—and I only touched ground three times between the Bottom and here!"

"I believe that," Coffey remarked, "in spite of your telling it, Morrow. But where I was, this blizzard hit the quickest and hardest of anywhere. The inspector sent me over to Beaver Lake this morning on one of these thank-you jobs for Indian Agent Duncan. The whitefish in the lake were cutting didos something fierce; you know how they jump up out of the water during rain or sleet, to see what's coming next. Well, one big boy—he must've weighed twenty pounds—flipped out and turned a somersault and started under again. But just then that first blast came roaring across the water, and it laid down skating ice. That big whitefish didn't quite make it back under the water. If you don't believe me, you can mosey over there and see his tail and hindquarters sticking out of the ice yet!"

"What a congergation of liars I got to live with!" Corporal Zsbyski growled, pulling off his boots and heavy clothing in anticipation of "bunk patrol" that afternoon. "But I admit that this is a dangerous blow to be out in. If she's all this cold with a gale howling, what'll she be when the wind lays and the still cold comes on? Does anybody know what happened with that bunch of spirit-wrestlers that was a-wandering around our district looking for the Promised Land?"

"Lay off the sarcastics, Zsbyski," Coffey objected, with some heat. "You've got no call to scoff at them Doukhobors. Their belief may be a mite queer, but they're dead earnest about it."

"Well then," Zsbyski came back, "God pity the poor sailors on the sea tonight. D'you object to that, Coffey?"

"I swear, Zy," Sergeant Pednault said, "you take the cake for blasphemery. When Gabriel blows his horn, you'll throw your bootjack at him for waking you up. Looky, if you don't mend your wicked ways, Agent Duncan is going to give it to you in the neck. He's complained about you to Division headquarters already."

Zsbyski flushed red. "D'you know my opinion about that mealy-mouthed hypocrite?"

"I do, Zy," said Pedneault. "And I'll double anything you say about him, so long as it's uncomplimentive. But that don't alter the fact that he's riding you and he's going to put you on the greased skids, unless you watch your step. But let's forget old Sour-Face. Dinner's all over, but we kept some hay and oats warm for you. Better hurry and tie into it. Soon as Morrow and me finish skinning this pair of cheaters, you and me have got to get in

Shepherd of the Storm 109

some practice with the boxing mitts. Nuttall says that if one of us don't win that Division boxing belt, he'll bust us both to buck cops."

In the boarded-off mess corner of the quarters Zsbyski swallowed several sweet potatoes candied with maple syrup, a hunk of moose jerky, bread with blueberry jam, and a mug of coffee. As he cocked his chair back and drank a second mug, he was thinking angrily about Mr. George M. Duncan, the Indian Agent at Lac Outarde Settlement. A thin-haired, dyspeptic man of forty, the Agent was called Sour-Face by the Indians and a variety of things by the other people of that frontier country. Duncan's predecessor, Forrest Ewing, had broken down under his severe labors a year before and had been replaced, but Duncan was in no danger of breaking down from overwork. He wore out no horses in the summer or dog teams in winter visiting his extensive territory. As Indian Agent, he was supposed to visit the different Indian bands and half-breed settlements and counsel them about crops, gardens, and livestock, and help them through this bad time when they were changing from the ways of nomad hunters to a more settled and secure existence. But instead of this he lived at Lac Outarde in his big, comfortable house and let the Cree bands get along as best they could. A political appointee with a pious, sanctimonious air about him, he was a dangerous man, who had political connections back East and knew how to use them craftily.

His hostility toward Corporal Zsbyski had started the

previous spring when the corporal, in his blunt way, had told the Agent that instead of sending out those bales of pious handbills to the Cree bands, he ought to be going around showing them how to grow gardens and milk a cow. The corporal's remarks had kindled Duncan's wrath, and ever since then the Agent had been out to get him kicked off the Force, on charges of profanity, irreligion, and pernicious example to the Indians.

Even Zsbyski's best friends had to admit that the charges had some appearance of being true. A rough-speaking, scoffing sinner, Zsbyski had spent his thirty-three years knocking around at a dozen different raw occupations. When occasion demanded he could cuss the bluest streak ever heard west of Winnipeg. Born on an immigrant ship coming from the North Baltic, he spoke three European tongues, besides English and French; and this fluency in five languages naturally lent color and punch to his speech. His several seasons in the Quebec sugarbush, his lobster-fishing trips on the Blue-Nose coast, his turns on a Newfoundland sealer, his mule-logging on the upper Saguenay, and his two years as a cavalry trooper in Montana—all this had gone into his rough, hard-hitting make-up.

Sucking a quill toothpick, Zsbyski strode out to the stove again and stood watching the euchre game. It was a neck-and-neck finish. In that last round Breden attempted to get Hightower's attention and pass him the right bower under the table. Pretending to scratch his shin, Sergeant Pedneault intercepted the pass and got the card himself. Breden half choked as the sergeant solemnly plumped down the bower on the board, captured the crucial trick, and won the game!

Constable Coffey had already cleared a space in the middle of the barracks and chalked a ring on the floor. Pedneault brought out the boxing gloves and tossed a pair to Zsbyski.

For three seasons straight Sergeant Pedneault had been boxing champion of the Western Division; and at Regina last year he had won top honors in the whole Mounted. His most serious opposition was right at home, in the hefty person of Gabriel Zsbyski. In a bare-knuckle fight Zsbyski's equals were few and far between, but in boxing something was wrong with him. Pedneault regularly outstepped, outboxed and outhit him, and yet the sergeant had a hunch that Zsbyski was a little the better man.

Amiable and easy-go-lucky, Pedneault was willing that Zsbyski should go down to Regina in his stead if the corporal stood the better chance at the belt. He and Zsbyski had gone through the "Awkward Squad" together, come west together and had been together for years. They had traded wallops in barracks practice, singed their whiskers fighting the same prairie fires, and had stood leg to leg in knock-down fights with turbulent *métis* when the latter got out of hand.

The practice that afternoon was the same story—Pedneault punched Zsbyski all over the ring. As Breden called time for the fourth round to start, the sergeant came out slowly, scratching his beard with his gloved thumb.

"I think I've puzzled out what's wrong with you, Zy. You're the kind of a boxer who's got to be either as cool as a cucumber or else mad as a grizzly on the prod. When you're cool you can box, and when you're mad you can hit like a mule kick. But you somehow keep just betwixt—"

They were interrupted. The door slammed open and Inspector Nuttall came in.

"I'm glad to see you're back, Zsbyski," the O.C. said, plainly relieved. "When you didn't show up this morning with the other men, I began to worry about you."

"I was delayed over at Loon Waddle Portage, sir," Zsbyski explained simply. "I had to straighten things up at Johnny Bad-Man's place."

The corporal did not give the details of straightening up the half-breed household, which were: thrashing Johnny Bad-Man sober, helping his wife put up a tin heating stove, running the cow, horse, and goat into the wolf pen, and making a jump-rabbit toy for the little Indian boy.

Nuttall looked thoughtfully at the chalked boxing ring and then at the cards scattered on the table. He motioned to his two non-coms and they followed him aside.

"It's no affair of mine," he told them, "how you men spend your off-duty time; you've little enough of it, goodness knows. I'm not objecting personally to your boxing in barracks or having a sociable game of cards, but it

Shepherd of the Storm   113

sounds deuced bad in a complaint. Especially against you, Zsbyski. I just received a sharp query about you from headquarters, and I don't quite know what to reply, because—well, some of Duncan's charges have some show of truth to them."

For the third time the door slammed open, and in came a middle-aged Cree who was doing thirty days about the post for setting out a prairie fire to drive game.

"Devil box jingle-jingle," he informed Nuttall.

The inspector turned up his coat collar and hurried off to his cabin. When he came back, his six men were sitting about the stove, thumbs in vest-holes, grumbling. The O.C.'s face was long, and a worried look stood in his eyes. The men straightened up on their chairs, knowing that something had gone badly wrong.

"The Hudson Bay man at Lac Outarde Settlement," Nuttall said tersely, "just called me over the Police line. He reports that those two hundred Doukhobors are caught in this blizzard seven miles north of the settlement and eleven miles northeast of here. They're at the wagon ford on Rivière Sans Sautes. They've got no tents, no winter clothes, and no gumption about weather like this."

"Great blue blazes!" Zsbyski spluttered. The other men were silent, in the silence of consternation.

Nuttall went on, "Those people can't last many hours in this blizzard—particularly the women and children. About the only hope is to get them back to shelter at Lac Outarde. I don't know if it's humanly possible to get through to them. Frankly, the chances are slim. I can't *order* any man of you to try it; the risk of getting lost and freezing to death is too heavy. But. . . ."

It was a call for a volunteer, and all six men knew it.

A silence gripped the barracks, save for the blizzard roaring down from the Arctic Barrens and screaming over the Mounted quadrangle. Breathing a little heavily, the men glanced at one another, shuffled their feet awkwardly—and said nothing. The ominous howling outside was a warning.

It was Corporal Zsbyski who broke the taut silence. His tilted chair came down with a thump.

"Hang it, I'll go! I just cain't let them poor souls freeze to death while I hug a stove or snooze around in my bunk. I'm the only one here can talk their lingo."

Sergeant Pedneault spoke up. "I'll go with you, Zy."

Zsbyski scowled and kicked a chair. "You stay blankety right here, Ped. In a storm like this'n we'd be hunting each other half the time. It's better for one man to have his own head and bust through. One man'll do as much good as a dozen. I'm the man to go and I'm going alone."

The constables began breathing easier. The O.C. looked at Pedneault. "Zsbyski is right, sergeant. Besides, you'll be needed here at the post. Corporal, get yourself ready and come over to my cabin. Immediately. We've got only a few hours of light at the most."

Zsbyski dressed quickly in clothes that were warm but not bundlesome. Carrying a pair of bear-paw racquets

Shepherd of the Storm

for the new snow, he left the barracks and crossed the quadrangle to Nuttall's cabin.

The inspector, fully dressed, was examining his racquet strings as Zsbyski came in. The corporal stared at him and blurted out, "Them fur duds you've got on, sir—what in consternation are they for?"

Nuttall said quietly, "I'm going along with you on this patrol. I don't ask for volunteers on any patrol that I myself won't face."

Corporal Zsbyski balked. He knew that one man stood as good a chance of getting through as two men. If he himself couldn't get through, his O.C. certainly couldn't either. Whatever happened, he would not need the inspector's help.

"You're not going and blast me you're not!" he snorted, balking flat-footed. "You're staying here and running the post."

"Since when," Nuttall demanded, "have you been the Officer Commanding around here?"

"It's not that I'm giving you any orders, sir. It's just that you're not going along. Horse sense is horse sense."

Inspector Nuttall slowly put down his racquets. He knew that when Corporal Gabriel Zsbyski balked, nothing short of a boulder avalanche could budge the man.

"Well," he said, "if you simply won't have it my way—"

"Not with butter and jam on!" Zsbyski grunted.

Nuttall took out his belt-gun, carefully wiped off the oil, and handed the weapon to the corporal. "Better take this, along with yours. Also, my gelding is already saddled up in the stable.

"Now look. If you do get through to the Doukhobors, I suggest that you lead them down the Sans Sautes Valley to the settlement. The deep valley will be a windbreak, and the frozen stream will make good level going. Now, a word about these Doukhobors. They're under the leadership of a big burly fellow who calls himself St. John the Apostle. He's led them into all sort of misery by wandering about looking for he doesn't know what. They believe and obey him implicitly. He's a fanatic and may cause you trouble if you don't handle him easy."

"I'll handle him," Zsbyski promised. "But I've got to be starting."

Nuttall laid a hand on the doorknob. His strait-laced manner dropped from him; he swallowed hard and held out his hand. "Corporal, I hope to heaven that—that you—"

"I'll get through, don't worry," Zsbyski reassured him, and flung out into the storm.

2

As he fought his way across the open quadrangle to the stable, he was appalled at the fury of the blizzard. He had known what he was bargaining for, but still he was daunted. He had to lean heavily forward against the gale.

Its savage coldness clutched at his breath and beat at him with its wings, like a living thing. It screamed at him, volleyed shot-hard pellets into his face, and lapped him in a blinding swirl of spume.

"She's *hiyu* wicked, all right!" he gasped, dodging into the stable. "But I've seen wickeder—blast me I have!"

This was a lie to keep up his nerve, and he knew it. He had never seen a worse blizzard; he had never seen its equal.

The Cree waiting inside was stoically rubbing snow on an ear which had been frosted when he came across from the cabin, thirty yards away. He helped Zsbyski with the gelding, and it was a job to get the horse out of the barn. The animal's instinct seemed to warn it against leaving the building. When the side door was opened, the horse snorted, jerked loose, and plunged back into its stall. But finally Zsbyski and the Cree coaxed and pulled it outside.

Zsbyski climbed into the saddle, headed the gelding into the blizzard, and spurred it forward.

The route from the Mounted post to Rivière Sans Sautes led across eleven miles of high, exposed prairie cut by four timbered valleys. The upland was buried under two feet of powder-fine snow and swept by changing, swirling windrows of drift. The deep valleys would give a little respite from the gale, but to a horse they were almost impassable. Floundering snowbanks filled them to the level of the lower limbs of the whitewoods; and their wind-swept eastern slopes were sheeted with ice from the rain just before the storm.

Coaxed and urged by Zsbyski, the gelding traversed a mile and a half in hopeful time, and they reached the first valley. But at the top of the icy slope the horse stopped short. Coaxing and spurring availed nothing. The animal pranced this way and that, smelling, snorting, and backing up from the icy edge.

Giving it a free rein because there was nothing else to do, Zsbyski began to suspect that the animal was figuring out some way of its own to get down the slope to the bottom. He was right. When it had thoroughly inspected the slope, it gingerly approached a slick place, planted its forefeet on the ice, drew its hind feet up carefully, braced all four legs, and started sliding. Horse and rider brought up more or less orderly in a snowbank down in the little valley.

The corporal knocked a path through the drifted bottom and led the horse across to the opposite slope. Sheltered from the wind, the slope was snow-covered but not drifted, and they got up it without great trouble.

Across the two miles to the next timber belt the gelding managed to butt its way through the gale. But the storm was breaking its nerve, and the ceaseless lash of the Arctic cold was driving it panicky. Zsbyski sympathized with the creature. It was new to the West; it had never faced a Saskatchewan blizzard; and he could understand the dumb, quivering terrors that the storm roused in it.

Shepherd of the Storm   119

At the next ice-sheeted slope the gelding pranced this way and that along the edge, refusing to try getting down the glass-smooth hill. After wasting many long minutes urging it, Zsbyski dismounted, took the bridle in his mitten, and attempted to lead the animal down. A sudden, reeling plunge of the horse tore the reins out of his hand; he slipped, lost his footing, and went careening down the slope till he fetched up in a jumble of half-buried boulders.

He got up, shook himself, and glanced up at the top, where the gelding was nowhere to be seen. "Not even any use scrambling back up there and looking," he muttered. "That poor critter is high-tailing it back to the post—and blast me if I blame him any."

When he groped around and found his racquets, he was staggered to see that the beam of one of them was broken. A broken racquet, in this savage blizzard, with miles yet to go to Rivière Sans Sautes. . . .

He drew off his mittens and gloves to mend the racquet, but before he could cut a leather strip from his boottops, his fingers were as numb and stiff as wooden pegs. Cursing his luck, he toed into the racquets, swung on down to the valley bottom and up the west slope, and ran into the teeth of the blizzard howling over the highland.

The rocky, saw-tooth hill range north of the post was like an instrument in the hands of the storm. Passes and high cliffs were stops and keys. From a low roaring to a shrill howl the blizzard blew through them in a dozen different storm-notes. It would lull for a moment, and the spume would lay; then it would strike a clublike blow, sometimes so sharp and hard that Zsbyski dropped on hands and knees till it kicked over.

Forty-seven degrees below zero, with winds that rose to sixty miles an hour—it seemed to Zsbyski that the country had been changed into an inferno, where all light and warmth and life had vanished. He had to breathe through the fur of his mittens, and even so, his lungs burned. He fought ahead cautiously, knowing that any struggle or exertion meant deep breathing, and this would bring the danger of frozen lungs. Unable to see any landmarks in the blanketing spume, he plowed along with eyes half closed, trusting to his instinct for guidance.

In the third timbered valley he stopped to rest. After lopping off an armful of spruce boughs, he scooped out a hole with his racquet, and threw the boughs in to sit on. In a general way he knew where he was, but before going on he chopped into several birches to make sure that his north and south were still straight, for he realized that any wasted steps might be fatal. Four miles still lay ahead of him, the snow was piling deeper, his left racquet had become a sorry excuse, and he would have the blizzard full in his teeth over those four endless miles.

It took an hour and a half to reach the next valley. His knees wobbled a bit as he stumbled and slid down the steep slope into the bottom spruces. An impulse seized him to plunge on at once; to tackle those last two

Shepherd of the Storm

miles and get them over with. But he made himself dig a hole as before and build a fire and rest, knowing that he would make time by stopping and would be surer of getting there at all.

When he climbed out of the valley into the storm and faced those last two miles, he wavered, stopped, and for the first time lost hold on his bulldog self. It seemed utterly impossible for any human to butt into that blizzard and live. Until then he had believed he had a chance to get through. Now he felt, without admitting it to himself, that the two miles were beyond his power.

In a numb, dogged way he tried to think. If he went back to his fire, banked snow for shelter, and dragged up wood enough to last the night, he probably could wait out the blizzard safely. Then he thought about the Doukhobors. Two hundred lives, among them women and helpless children; two hundred people depending solely on him. . . .

He bent his head low, groaned at his aching left leg, and started on toward Rivière Sans Sautes.

At the end of a mile he felt exhaustion creeping over him. Back to the wind, he crouched a minute in the snow to rest. Almost instantly he was half covered with drift. He shook it off, got up, and shoved ahead. He had to rest again within a few hundred yards. The next time he made a hundred yards by sheer nerve. The next, only fifty.

It was harder and harder to shake off the drift and

battle on. Without his realizing it, the intervals of rest grew longer, longer.

The time came when Zsbyski could not drive himself forward. Though he managed to get up, his left leg gave way under him, and he sank back. The steady, sibilant *seesh-seesh-seesh* of the driven snow lulled his senses. While the warm drift piled up at his back, he stared dully and helplessly at the dancing, wraithlike whirls of spume that whipped past him and went scudding out of sight down the gale.

Presently, between the dancing swirls, he made out a long blackish shadow twenty paces away, on his back trail. It was *not* a snow wraith. It was sitting still, its nose raised, its head tilted sideways.

Behind it Zsbyski thought he saw others. He rubbed the frost from his eyelashes and then he saw the shadowy things distinctly—ten others. They were waiting patiently, as if they had waited thus before.

A jolt of anger surged through Corporal Zsbyski. The wolves jerked him back to his senses when nothing else could have. He got to his feet, shook his mittened fist at the gray forms and swore at them. The wolves backed up out of range and sat down again.

But not Zsbyski. He lowered his head once more and battled into the storm. Whenever he slowed down or his will started slipping, he turned and looked back through the spume at the eleven big timber wolves. His numbed brain was aware of just two things—that wolf pack behind him and the valley shelter somewhere close ahead.

He reached the Sans Sautes slope so abruptly that he lost his footing and rolled down nearly to the bottom flat. The low-sweeping branches of a giant basswood stopped him. In spite of its ice coating he recognized the tree; it was barely four hundred yards above the ford. He dusted himself off, and limped down the frozen, level stream. After his battle with the wind, the going was easy, and in ten minutes he was at the crossing.

To his utter amazement, there was not a sign of the Doukhobors or their camp anywhere around.

In blank bewilderment he leaned against a sapling, rubbed the frost from his eyes, and peered all around through the murky gloom. There was no mistake, this was the crossing—he himself had helped chop that swath through the lodge-pole timber on both sides of the stream.

He shouted in Russian. Nobody answered. He saw nothing, heard nothing; and it finally came home to him that the Doukhobors had simply not camped at the Rivière Sans Sautes ford.

Baffled and furious, Zsbyski sat down on a broken sapling and opened his lips and spoke. He wore out five languages in ten minutes. He ripped Factor Hewes McAulay up the back for reporting that the Doukhobors were there at the crossing. He gave Nuttall a currycombing for asking a person to go get them. He keelhauled himself for risking his life and battling through eleven miles of blizzard, all for nothing. He gave the Doukhobors a lip-larruping for wandering around in a Saskatchewan woolly-whipper instead of staying in the Ukraine where they belonged.

Feeling considerably relieved, he gathered wood and coaxed a fire to burn, took off his mittens under its protection, and set to work on his racquet. As he worked he tried to think.

It would be dark within an hour. By morning the temperature would hit sixty-five below zero. Men, women and children, the Doukhobors would freeze to death, wherever they were.

The thought tormented him. His racquet mended, he got up and hunted around for signs that the Doukhobors had used the crossing just before the storm, but the snow had buried everything. The question throbbed in his brain: where in the *blank-blank-blank were* those Doukhobors? Factor Hewes McAulay had said they were at the Sans Sautes ford. By Little Mother Volga and the Great Horn Spoon this *was* that very ford. So, McAulay had made a mistake.

But the immigrant band, Zsbyski reasoned, simply had to be somewhere north of Lac Outarde, and not far away. Coming north from the settlement, they probably had kept to the freight-hauler trail up the valley; the soaking rain had made the prairies almost impassable to their man-drawn carts. They hadn't gone on north up the main valley or the Johnny Bad-Man household would have seen them. The only branch trail led up Little Sans Sautes. Could they have taken that? There was an old

Shepherd of the Storm

buffalo wallow on Little Sans Sautes that sometimes was called a ford. Maybe that's where they were.

It was the only possibility Zsbyski could think of. In spite of his near-exhaustion, he decided to go and see.

As he put on his racquets he noticed that the wolves, which had been inching closer and closer in the slow twilight, were sitting in a semicircle not thirty feet away. He thought: "You're getting too familiar, you hungry cusses. Guess I'll give you a dressing down before I hightail it for Little Sans Sautes crossing."

After kicking snow over the fire, he shuffled down the frozen stream a hundred yards and stopped suddenly behind a jutting rock. When the pack came loping around the jut, they met with a hot surprise, and three of them sprawled in the snow at the burst from Zsbyski's belt-gun.

At a long, swinging shuffle he hurried down the valley, looking over his shoulder at times. He came to the forks, turned up Little Sans Sautes and headed on for the old buffalo wallow.

A quarter mile away from it he halted sharply, listening to a queer low sound. It seemed to him like people singing. Like a chorus of many, many people. In a lull between the savage blasts of the blizzard he heard it distinctly—a hundred-voiced chant that rose and fell with the fury of the storm.

He leaned forward and fought his way toward the pathetic, low-toned chant of the wanderers.

3

Zsbyski's arrival at the Doukhobor camp was the most spectacular entrée he had ever made in his thirty-three years. During his years with the Mounted he had sneaked up on many a nest of "permit" runners and had broken up many a secret blood-dance, but this arrival seemed to him the beat of them all. It was a pure accident, and as much a surprise to him as to the Doukhobors themselves, but nonetheless it was more impressive than trumpets and a fanfare.

To save time he had cut across an open highland where the river made an oxbow. As he neared the camp the chanting stopped, and the veering wind fooled him. In the swirling darkness he hit the little valley above the camp, turned around, and started downstream. The wind at his back whooped him along, and the way he went down that valley reminded him of how Constable Morrow had spread his coattails and flown home. A vicious, high-screaming gust of wind blanketed him in swirling snow and dropped him precipitately over a jump-off into the very center of the camp.

If he had been charioted out of the clouds, his arrival could hardly have been more startling.

The jump-off he had dropped over was the snow-buried Doukhobor carts, which had been thrown to-

Shepherd of the Storm

gether in a square with one side open. In one corner of this miserable shelter the Doukhobors were kneeling together in a huddle, praying. They had no fires, for Little Sans Sautes had burned off that summer; and their clothes were pitifully inadequate for the Saskatchewan blizzard. There were eighty men, roughly clad, and eighty young peasant wives, their heads and arms wrapped in coarse gray shawls. The rest of the two hundred were children, most of them under three, many of them born enroute from the Old Country, as Zsbyski himself had been born.

In the center of the group their leader, a huge, wild-eyed fanatic, stood bareheaded with arms upraised, leading the chant, as his followers slowly froze.

In stupefied amazement the Doukhobors stared at Zsbyski as he fairly dropped out of the storm into their camp and appeared before them. The leader stopped waving his arms; the chanting broke off; even the crying of the children was for a moment hushed. Zsbyski himself realized what a strange figure indeed he must be in their eyes! He was snow-plastered; the whiskers on his rocky chin were frosted—he looked more like a storm-specter than a flesh-and-blood human.

A pock-scarred man sprang wildly to his feet and leveled an arm toward Zsbyski. "Did I not prophesy to ye, brothers—?"

The rest of his sentence was flung down the wind. Before he could repeat his words, the huge leader struck him with a clenched fist and knocked him sprawling.

Zsbyski had utterly no idea what all this meant. But he wasted little time wondering. His first glance told him that the women and children were in pitiful condition.

"Get up!" he bade the group in their own tongue. "Get up and follow me. I have come to lead you to shelter. You will die here. Get up and follow. Quickly."

Expecting them to snatch at his offer, he was dumfounded when not a soul of the two hundred stirred. All of them turned their eyes upon their leader and silently awaited his answer.

"Who are ye?" he challenged Zsbyski hoarsely, in a Scriptural chant. "With what temptation, O unholy one, would ye tempt these people who are my children? It was by the Word that I brought them here, and here shall they stay until the Word comes to me to lead them hence."

The Doukhobors groaned, but not a voice was raised in opposition to the leader. Zsbyski smelled trouble. He could see that the leader's fiat of power over his followers was no idle boast. The fellow's domination was absolute; they would obey him in the face of death. These were a hard-minded people, of blind faith and a grim, terrible earnestness. As the man bade them do, so would they do.

Then, with a jolt, Zsbyski remembered Nuttall's warning that he might have trouble with their fanatic leader, who believed that the spirit of St. John the Apostle had wrestled with his body and taken possession thereof.

"Holy brass bells!" he thought. "Getting here was a tough enough job, but now look what a crick I'm up!"

He hid his anger and desperate impatience, and tried to conciliate the huge leader. "Nay," he said to the man, "you heard my words wrong, captain of souls. Surely you shall lead these children, your followers. I am sent only as a guide, to bring you to shelter. But if you stay here, how many of you will the morning find alive? Would you have your children die here tonight?"

A chorus of groans burst from the men and women, as if in answer to the corporal's question. It was a mute, wordless prayer to their leader to deliver them from their suffering.

But Zsbyski's words and the groans were a challenge to the huge leader. He clenched his fists high over his head and shouted to his flock till their pleas died to a murmur and the murmur itself finally hushed. His power over the huddled, freezing band made Zsbyski's blood run cold.

"Into a new land have I led my people," the fellow chanted in a booming, exultant voice. "From their heavy labor and their bondage unto wicked kings have I led them; yea, from the land of iniquities to the land which the Great Father has promised me for my children. Shall ye then cast an eye backwards? Much less shall ye return one step! Here we shall stay, and when our tribulations cease, then shall our eyes behold the land that was promised to us."

The pock-scarred man again leaped to his feet, leveling

an accusing arm at the leader. "Ye are false!" he shouted, stamping his broken shoes. "It is not the Apostle John that possesses you, but a devil! Yea, a devil; a devil!" He whirled to the other Doukhobors. "Did I not tell ye, brothers? Did I not prophesy that one would come who would be possessed of a true prophet and would deliver us?"

Again the leader swung his fist at the pock-marked Doukhobor, but this time his rival evaded him.

Zsbyski had only a hazy notion what the strange clash meant between the two men. He did not much care what it meant. To him the only thing that mattered was that the women and children were freezing to death. He said quietly to the leader, "But your people will die here tonight. I am a guide sent to take you and your followers to shelter. . . ."

"Ye are a fiend!" the huge fellow blared at him. "Begone! Go before the wrath of an apostle scorches ye!"

Zsbyski backed up a step from the man's fiery denunciation. He thought that surely his ears must be playing tricks with him. The leader's queer combination of power and madness—power over so many other people, and madness that would lead to their deaths—was something he had never seen before.

He tried again, pointing out the plight of the band and the haven he could take them to. The big leader shouted him down with, "No! Fiend! Begone!"

In desperation Zsbyski spoke past him to the Doukhobors themselves. He pleaded, threatened, ordered. But all the results he got was a moaning for the shelter and warmth that he described. With sinking heart he realized that they would stick with their leader. As long as the fanatic kept his spell over their minds and was an apostle in their eyes, just that long there would be no budging them.

The big fellow was advancing on him menacingly. "Ye fiend, ye cheat, ye devil—trying my followers' faith in me!" he thundered, in a dangerous fury at Zsbyski for talking to the Doukhobors over his head. "Begone, or I will rend you limb from limb!"

Zsbyski stopped backing up. His anger was kindling. Reason and soft words were not his long suit and they had failed, anyhow. To be called a cheat and a devil, not to mention some of the epithets that were untranslatable, was more than he had ever taken from anybody, and now he was vowing to take no more of them from this fanatic. But what really angered him was the idea of a self-appointed "apostle" keeping him from saving the two hundred people he had been sent to save. So he stopped flat-footed, took a deep breath, and opened up on his enemy.

He committed the man to seven bottomless pits and a dozen purgatories. He ran through the roll call of Eastern Devils. He swore that the apostle was a cloven-hoofed cheat, a horned liar, a fork-tailed impostor. "And by the beard of St. Boris," he wound up, smacking a fist into his mitten, "if you are the Apostle John, I am Gabriel himself and your better."

At the corporal's words the pock-marked man jumped wildly to his feet, shouting and thrashing his arms. The murmur among the Doukhobors swelled to a hoarse outcry.

Without knowing what or why, Zsbyski saw that his words had touched off something drastic. He saw, furthermore, that the issue between him and the leader was coming to a head, and coming fast. Bending down, he loosened his racquets so that he could step out of them quickly.

Roaring with rage at the stinging lash of Zsbyski's tongue, the apostle lunged forward. "Ye fiend, I shall break thy bones and dissolve thee!"

Ordinarily Zsbyski would have been the apostle's match in a stand-up fight, even though the apostle was much stronger, bigger, and longer-armed. But the five solid hours of battling a blizzard had nearly exhausted him. He wanted to get the fight over with in a hurry. Meeting the charge squarely, he stepped in between the huge arms outflung to grasp him and planted a short uppercut on the man's jaw. It snapped up the apostle's head, as he had figured, and he followed through with a terrific, long-swinging right on the tilted chin. It was not enough. It stopped the apostle's bull charge, but otherwise scarcely fazed him.

Then and there Zsbyski realized that only shrewd, cool boxing could bring him through this battle. The thought jigged through his mind that he was fighting not only for his own life against an infuriated, bearlike man, but for

Shepherd of the Storm

the lives of two hundred people. Sternly he got a grip on himself and took stock. He had fought brute fighters before. The strategy always was to wear them down; to keep away from them; keep jabbing and hammering them; keep tying 'em in knots—and always keep cool yourself. Cool as a cucumber, like Pedneault said.

He felt almost as though his loyal partner were standing ghostily just back of him and saying, "Cool, cool, Zy. Cool as a cucumber—or he'll murder you. Don't let him grapple; you're too bad fagged for that. Easy does it, Zy; easy and cool."

Deliberately he began to whittle his enemy down. As he backed off, he dug in a short-rib punch that made the apostle gasp. The latter charged again. Still Zsbyski backed off, saving his strength while he landed shrewd, weakening punches, and boxing off the long-swinging, murderous blows aimed for him. Coolly he kept playing for the stomach and short ribs. For the first time in his fighting days he landed when and where he pleased.

In a few minutes of hot work he had the apostle breathing like an engine piston. The lunges were weakening; the murderous blows were fewer and not so murderous.

At the right moment Zsbyski failed to back up from a lunge. He stepped in between the arms again and planted the preliminary left uppercut. Then his long, bone-smashing right landed on the tilted jaw. The apostle sagged limply and fell forward against him. Zsbyski let him tumble into the snow.

"I don't know how I'd fight if I got bull-mad," he panted, as he drew the mittens on over his raw knuckles, "but old Ped was dead right about me keeping cool as a cucumber!"

He turned to the Doukhobors and raised a hand to still them. A howling blast kicked over, leaving a few seconds of taut quiet in its wake. But before he could speak, the pock-scarred man was on his feet again, gesticulating and shouting himself hoarse. In the silence, with no huge fist to knock him down, his words to the immigrant band rang clear and startling.

"Have I not told ye that the leader ye followed was a false leader? Did I not tell ye that he was leading ye into destruction? Did I not prophesy that a major saint would appear among us and deliver us? Lo! he is come! He hath confounded the impostor and lo! he hath stilled the storm. From his own lips ye have heard his name. Let us arise and take up our goods and do as he biddeth!"

Zsbyski's mouth dropped open with astonishment. The words about his being a major saint and a deliverer from on high struck him like a cartload of bricks, and he leaned feebly against a wagon wheel. By the strangeness of his arrival, by his scoffing jest about being St. Gabriel, by his hard-won victory over the apostle, by everything he had said and done he had played right into the stark-mad prophecy! He had led himself to the slaughter! Now he understood the strange play between the two men. And why the Doukhobors, at his arrival, had stared at him as if he were either a devil or an angel.

"St. Gabriel—*me!*" he gasped. He sat down weakly on a wagon tongue, while the pock-scarred man danced about triumphantly at the fulfillment of his prophecy. Zsbyski watched him in amazement. "Me—St. Gabriel!" He thought about his six rough-tough comrades at the barracks. "If they ever hear about this, ever hear that I was supposed to be St. Gabriel—oh, oh, oh!"

Presently he straightened up and looked around at his flock. Whether they really believed he was a major saint he could not tell, but now that he had confounded their false apostle they plainly did believe that he had been divinely sent to deliver them from their suffering and guide them to haven. In their manner toward him, and on their countenances too, their unquestioning belief in him was clearly written.

He looked at them and saw that all their eyes were upon him. In the face of a trust like theirs he could neither mock nor laugh. A queer feeling of awe crept over him—of awe of his heavy responsibility and their simple, genuine religious faith. However blind their faith might be, it was genuine.

Quietly and quickly he gave his orders to the band of wanderers. They formed in fours, with strong men in front to break a path and other men at the rear to help the weaker ones along. The carts and all equipment were abandoned; there would be time to recover them when the blizzard stopped. In less than five minutes he had the band out of the camp and was leading them down the valley of Little Sans Sautes.

The men breaking the path in front had to be relieved by others every few minutes. The women trudged along silently, bearing their sufferings without a moan. Both men and women were exhausted, numb with cold, weak with hunger, and almost ready to give up the struggle; and Zsbyski could keep them moving only by desperate exertions. He himself was stumbling with fatigue, but his responsibility for those two hundred souls gave him strength, and their faith in him as their shepherd buoyed him up.

But the procession made such slow time in the cold and windy blackness that at the Big Sans Sautes forks, where he allowed them to halt for a brief rest, he debated whether to stop and camp there, out of the storm, and try to build fires. He doubted if he could ever get his band the few miles on to Lac Outarde Settlement. But he decided that he had to go on with them willy-nilly. When the storm laid and the still cold tightened down, open fires would not be enough. Without blankets or any good heavy clothing, the women and children would never live through it. They had to have shelter and food quickly.

While his band rested, he groped around in a stance of pine, found a dead tree, and with his hand-ax chopped a dozen splits out of it for torches. After lighting the splits and passing them back along the procession, he gave the word to march.

The spell of their strange religious faith moved Zsbyski profoundly. In all his life he had experienced nothing like it. Nor had he ever even imagined a situation as outlandish and bizarre as the one he was actually in. "St. Gabriel—*me!*" he would mutter, and would look around and rub his eyes to make sure that the glimmering torches were actual. It seemed to him a fantastic piece of irony that he, the most notorious, hard-swearing sinner of the whole Division, should be marching at the head of a Doukhobor band as their leader and shepherd—accepted by them as a heaven-sent guide in their hour of need.

As he coaxed and drove them on and on down the Sans Sautes valley, he hated more and more to trudge back along that line of stumbling, pitiful humans. They were suffering so dreadfully. All along the column they kept imploring him to intercede for them with the Great Father and say that their anguish was more than they could bear. And solemnly, to encourage them, Zsbyski promised. And where the suffering was particularly desperate and courage flickering out, he would close his bloodshot eyes and pray aloud for them, and say that the Great Father would soon bring their dolorous journey to an end.

4

Zsbyski brought his little band into Lac Outarde an hour after midnight. How to get them all into shelter quickly, at the tiny hamlet of a dozen houses, was the next problem.

In front of Agent Duncan's residence, a spacious two-story frame, he halted the procession and knocked at the door. He had to knock several times before Duncan appeared. Zsbyski explained the situation briefly and asked the Agent to take twenty of them.

"*Twenty?*" Duncan echoed, his teeth chattering. "My good man, how in the world can I accommodate twenty people? It's impossible! I can take two; no, I shall take three. But twenty. . . ."

"You don't understand," Zsbyski interrupted. "I've got two hundred people out here, freezing, and there's only a dozen houses to put them in. Your house is the biggest of all. . . ."

"But I tell you I can't take in twenty people and feed them and keep them warm and all that. I've told you that twenty is impossible."

"It's not a question of comfort," Zsbyski pleaded. "It's a question of their getting under a roof or freezing to death. Will you take fifteen then?"

"My good man, I told you I would take three. That is what I meant. Do I have to stand here and freeze repeating that?"

Zsbyski stared at the Agent, and a rage took hold of him. His big hands slowly clenched and unclenched. When he spoke, his voice was husky with fury.

"Get back to bed, you! I won't leave any of them here! I'd rather they'd freeze to death than stay under the roof of a mealy-mouthed hypocrite like you!"

Agent Duncan stiffened with shock and outrage. "Sirruh!" he spluttered. "Sir-ruh! You will rue—"

"For half a cent," Zsbyski blazed, "I'd rue you a good 'un on the jaw. Now get back to bed before I get mad and break every bone in your body!"

He turned to his band and led them on and stopped by the three houses of the Hudson Bay establishment. At his thundering kick, Factor McAulay thrust his head out of an upstairs window. Again Zsbyski started to explain, but he barely got the first words from his mouth.

"Great snakes!" the factor spluttered, catching sight of the long blur of figures behind the corporal. "Wait till I jerk my pants on, Zy. Shoot about thirty into here and forty into my trading store and a couple dozen into the warehouse. While you're getting the others quartered I'll whoop up fires and thaw these folk out and get something hot inside 'em!"

As the window came down with a bang, Zsbyski caught fragments of Hewes McAulay's excited words to his missus: "Sarah, wake up—heaven's sake—Corporal Zsbyski out there, with them Doukhobors. Sixty below zero—women and kids. . . . Woman, hurry up! . . ."

At one o'clock the next afternoon, through a still, bright cold of sixty-odd degrees below zero, three men loped out of the southeast prairie and racqueted into the open quadrangle of the Police post. They were Sergeant Pedneault, Constable Coffey, and Corporal Gabriel Zsbyski.

Pedneault and Coffey headed for the barracks, but Zsbyski crossed to Nuttall's cabin, knocked, and entered.

"Everything's lined up pretty well with the Doukhobors, sir," he reported to the inspector. "We scattered 'em around to the cabins, like I phoned; but McAulay has still got sixty on his hands. McAulay isn't a rich man, and I don't see how he's going to charge the expense against the Bay—"

"We have a government fund at our disposal for such purposes," Nuttall interrupted. "McAulay will get reimbursed. About these Doukhobors, are you sure they won't pick up and wander off again before we get a location for them?"

"I'm tolerable certain, sir. I talked around with 'em this morning, and I think they're about burned out on apostles and saints. They realized that it was this apostle and his ravings that caused all their troubles. He isn't exactly a real Doukhobor, but belongs to a special sect. But I'm positive he's done for with those people. His press-teege is flatter'n a pancake with them. And this pock-marked fellow, Ilyon—he's one of that special sect, too, with his own line of prophecies and ravings."

"So I heard," Nuttall remarked, suppressing a smile. "In fact, I understand that St. Gabriel is loose here in Saskatchewan."

Zsbyski turned brick red and clenched a fist. "If I catch who's peddling it around about last night," he growled, "I'll hit him so hard he'll wake up with a halo on."

Inspector Nuttall turned to the stove and stuck in

Shepherd of the Storm 141

some wood, meanwhile straightening up his face. When he came back to his desk he was serious and worried.

"Zsbyski," he said, "next spring and summer there'll be several thousand of these Doukhobors coming to the western Provinces to settle. Headquarters is looking around for a man who can take charge of the bands as they arrive, and guide them to their locations. But men who speak their language, know this country, and have gumption enough to handle their odd sort are scarce. The job carries a sergeancy. I would like to recommend you for it, and push you, Zsbyski; but. . . ."

"But what, sir?"

"Well, bluntly, headquarters won't go along with me, as things stand. They've had a series of complaints against you and they seem to think you're a pretty bad egg."

Zsbyski's face grew long. "You don't have to tell me who made those complaints," he said. "I guess that the sergeancy is really cooked now, after the hog-scalding I gave Duncan last night." He turned to the door. "I do thank you, sir, for wanting to recommend me, but just forget it. Some ways, I guess, Agent Duncan is right enough. I've been a pretty rough-tough specimen and a bad example."

Nuttall watched him leave. "Lord, a bad example!" he thought, picturing that heroic and incredible trek of last night.

Half an hour later a belled dog team pulled up at the inspector's cabin. Agent George M. Duncan emerged from the blankets and buffalo robes and hurried inside, his thin face hard, his eyes vengeful. Barely nodding to Nuttall's "How d'you do, Mr. Duncan," he demanded abruptly, "Inspector, you've got to suspend this Corporal Zsbyski from duty and see to it that he's discharged from the Mounted Police. Immediately, sir. I'll brook no delay."

Nuttall whistled under his breath. He asked drily, "Would you mind letting me know the basis of your demand?"

"He is a profane, blasphemous scoundrel!" Duncan rapped. "His influence in this region nullifies all my labors with the Indians. I've borne with him patiently till now, but when he comes to my house at midnight during a blizzard and insults me, vilifies me, threatens me. . . ."

Nuttall jerked a little. "What's this? Last night? He mentioned something—but just what did happen between Zsbyski and you last night?"

"Why, when he brought that band of fanatics to the settlement, he banged on my door and ordered me to take in twenty of them. When I refused, he became abusive and threatened me with physical violence. His exact words—I have them written down—were, 'Break every bone in your body.'"

Nuttall winced, and his face paled. He believed Duncan; the quotation was definitely Zsbyski-esque. His heart sank as he realized how such a threat against the Agent would sound to the Division superintendent, on top of the other charges. Zsbyski wouldn't get those three stripes. He wouldn't even keep his two stripes. He would probably be put off the Force summarily.

"I'm terribly sorry to hear this, Mr. Duncan," he said. "I apologize personally for the incident. I'm sure the corporal didn't really mean. . . . You see, he was exhausted from twelve hours of fighting a terrific blizzard, and he had on his hands two hundred people who needed shelter without a minute's delay. And maybe he didn't believe that twenty was a preposterous number, considering that the half-breeds, with their little two-room shacks, took in eight or ten apiece. . . ."

"You are upholding him, sirruh!" Duncan rasped. "Very well! I will see to it myself. Very well indeed, sirruh. I do not need your cooperation. I have other recourses."

He started for the door. But Nuttall stepped in front of him. "Just a minute, my Christian friend," the inspector snapped. His cheekbones were red, and his eyes flashed fire. All his long, patient program to keep down trouble dropped away. "If you've just got to have war, you can have it, and I'll see that you get plenty.

"During your year here, my overworked men and I have gone out of our way to help you on a hundred different occasions. Instead of being grateful, you write secret letters complaining about my post, and because of a personal grudge you've been gunning for one of my best men. All right! From now on, Agent Duncan, you'll conduct your affairs without help from us. How you'll get along with these Crees when we quit propping you up—that's going to be worth watching!

"Second point. I hear that Forrest Ewing, your predecessor, is well enough to return to Lac Outarde, if the Agency were vacant. All of us want him back. He established schools and taught. He persuaded the *métis* to quit their miserable freighting and take up land to farm. He went the rounds with my patrols, week in and week out—an old man, mind you. And now, what's *your* record? You've let his school work go to smash. You've let the *métis* slip back into their old ways. You won't learn Cree, so you have to deal through an interpreter.

"Just one more thing. I'm going to write up all these charges against you. I'm going to send copies to the Police heads, your Department chief, and the Eastern papers. You're always hinting around about secret influences and pulling wires. All right! It's a dirty business, but I've got secret influences too, and I can pull plenty wires. Now, suppose you jingle back home."

Duncan stood with his hand on the doorknob. Beneath the man's livid anger, Inspector Nuttall saw that he was shaken and afraid, and the officer breathed a silent prayer of thankfulness. He had played boldly, had spoken with a great deal more assurance than he felt, but now he saw that he was on solid ground.

As a parting fillip he told Duncan, "If you want to withdraw those sneak reports against Corporal Zsbyski and if you decide that this raw West is no place for you, Mr. Duncan, it might be that I wouldn't write up these charges. You don't have to answer right now, but think it over—and don't wait too long. . . ."

A few minutes later Sergeant Pedneault knocked at the door and entered. His left eye was puffed up suspiciously and his nose leaned a little to larboard. Inspector Nuttall looked at him questioningly.

"What's the matter, sergeant? What happened to you?"

"I was just boxing, Zsbyski and me. Practicing for that tournament. It's about Zsbyski that I wanted to talk to you, sir. Something queer has got into him."

"Good heavens, what's the trouble with that big hunk now? What else has he got into?"

"It's the way he acts, sir," Pedneault said. "He's been so queer and quiet. For one thing, he hasn't let out a single jawbreaker all day. He's not sick, and I can't figure what's come over him."

"I'll try to find out," Nuttall promised. "Anything else?"

"Yes, sir. It's about this matter of who goes to Regina for the boxing tournament. I believe Zy is the better man, and we ought to send him instead of me."

"That's unselfish of you, Pedneault. But I can't agree. I've seen you two boxing, and you're the better man by a good margin."

"That's what I used to think," Pedneault said ruefully. "Always before, I slammed Zy around the ring any old way. He's got stuff, but he wouldn't stay cool nor would he get fighting mad. So in our practice today, sir, seeing that he was quiet and not very lively during the first two rounds, I thought I'd jolly him up a little bit. So I said to him, 'Put up your mitts, St. Gabriel; I want to knock the halo off you!'"

Inspector Nuttall forgot to smoke. "Heavens! Then what?"

Pedneault rubbed at his swollen jaw. "Why, sir, considering all that happened to me right after that—well, that's how I know that Zy is the better man!"